THE SPIDER:
THE MILL-TOWN MASSACRES

THE MILL-TOWN MASSACRES

By Grant Stockbridge

STEEGER BOOKS • 2020

PUBLISHING HISTORY

"The Mill-Town Massacres" originally appeared in the February 1937 (Vol. 11, No. 1) issue of *The Spider* magazine. Copyright 2020 by Argosy Communications, Inc. All rights reserved.

CHAPTER 1
THE MASTER OF THE MADMEN

THE FIRST sign of trouble in the steel industry came when Big Harry Silvestro went berserk. Big Harry was the foreman of the night shift in the Number Three open hearth shop of the Keystone Iron and Steel Corporation, in the town of Keystone. He had held this job for five years, with never a single day out for sickness. Indeed, a glimpse of his stocky, powerful body, stripped to the waist as he worked, would have made anyone doubt that he could ever be sick.

He was regarded by the superintendent as a plodding, loyal, dependable man. For three years, the unit of which he was foreman had consistently won the inter-shop pool for the greatest production of ingots.

He had a wife and four children. He did not drink, smoke or chew. His square, almost bovine face topped by close-cropped black hair gave no indication that an original thought had ever entered his brain. But he could work, and he could make his men work. He did not seem to have a nerve in his body, and he never grew angry or flew off the handle. No one ever suspected that Big Harry Silvestro could grow excited or temperamental about anything.

Nevertheless, at two o'clock on Saturday morning, Big Harry went berserk.

It happened while a batch of molten steel was being poured

from one of the open hearth furnaces into the huge cylindrical bucket which would conduct the steel by the traveling crane across the shop to deposit it into a row of molds where it would cool into oblong ingots.

Silvestro was directing the operation, when suddenly he doubled over with pain. Both his great hands pressed hard against his abdomen, and a cold sweat broke out on his face and naked torso.

The sizzling molten steel was pouring in a thin stream, glistening silvery, and was spreading heat in every direction. Silvestro groaned, and pressed at his stomach, still doubled over. The

THE MILL-TOWN MASSACRES

The Spider's blazing guns came to the aid of the stricken guards.

men of his crew could not go to his assistance because they were handling the hot steel.

But Jack Markos, the little timekeeper, who happened to be passing through the shop at the moment, saw Big Harry's agony, and ran to his side, put a hand on the big man's shoulder.

"Harry!" he shouted. "What's the matter with you?"

Big Harry didn't answer. Instead, he straightened with a tremendous effort, and turned suddenly red-rimmed eyes at little Jack Markos. Markos looked up at him, and the little man's face went white at the stark madness that he saw in Silvestro's eyes. His jaw fell open, and he took an involuntary step backward, half turned to run.

But he was too late. Big Harry uttered a dreadful cry of mad rage, leaped after Markos, and seized the little man around the waist. Markos screamed, strained ineffectually, as Silvestro lifted him high in the air and hurled his diminutive body straight into the huge bucket of molten steel!

Markos' shrill scream died in a gurgling of agony drowned by the bubbling, sizzling steel. Dense fumes spurted from the bucket, as the steady stream of liquid metal continued to pour into it from the open hearth, to cover what was left of Jack Markos. He had been cremated alive.

A sudden hush descended upon the shop as the men stood in petrified horror. Markos was finished.

BIG HARRY SILVESTRO stood panting at the spot from which he had hurled Marko's body. His big chest was heaving and the breath was coming from his throat in great gasps. Saliva dribbled at his mouth, and his eyes were those of a madman. He stood half crouched, and the corded muscles of his stomach rippled with each breath he took. Apparently the pain was gone from his abdomen.

The men turned terrified stares upon him, hardly crediting the dreadful thing they had seen. That Harry Silvestro, their big, placid-tempered boss,—should suddenly become a murderer in the twinkle of an eye seemed incredible to them. At first their brains refused to accept the fact.

Then, as they realized that a murderer stood before them, their brows clouded, and they slowly began to advance, encircling Big Harry.

The huge bucket into which the steel was still pouring over Jack Markos' body was forgotten. They had all loved the little timekeeper, and a dull anger began to grow in them.

Big Harry Silvestro watched them close in on him, with eyes that reflected the cunning of madness. He began to back away, and Mike Foley, the operator of the overhead crane, shouted to the men from his booth: "He's mad! Watch out for him!"

Foley seized a huge monkey wrench, leaped from his booth, and ran toward Silvestro.

Big Harry's lips turned back from his teeth in a vicious snarl. The black hair that almost completely covered his chest glistened with perspiration. His tremendously long, gorilla-like arms stretched out toward the nearest of the advancing men, and he hunched forward as if to seize him. Mike Foley was only ten feet away from Silvestro, and he shouted: "Get out of the way! He'll throw you in!"

Big Harry lunged at the nearest man, and his arm twined

about the unfortunate fellow's waist. He lifted the man bodily from the floor, then his huge shoulder muscles bulged with the effort of raising the man high above his head, just as he had raised Jack Markos.

Then the other men closed in upon him, and they leaped at Silvestro, smashing at him with their fists, kicking at him with their feet. Mike Foley lunged in through the crowd, holding the monkey wrench high in the air, ready to bring it down on Silvestro's head.

But though these steel workers were powerful men themselves, Big Harry loomed above them all like a giant. Their blows and their kicks seemed to have little effect upon the crazed foreman. The man whom he had lifted into the air was struggling, squirming and shrieking, attempting to claw at his captor, and raking Big Harry's arms with grimy fingernails. Big Harry seemed to feel no pain at all.

The whole shop had stopped work, and all the men were rushing toward the wild scene. Big Harry tried to throw his man toward the seething cauldron of steel, but the workers were packed close about him, shouting and striking.

Suddenly the huge bucket overflowed, and the hot, molten metal began to sizzle on the floor, flowing out in fiery liquid streams along the floor. It was unnoticed by the milling throng around the big foreman. Mike Foley yelled: "Drop that man, Silvestro! I say, drop him!"

Silvestro snarled, and let go of the man, who dropped among

his crowding fellows. Big Harry swung around, both huge fists flailing out at his attackers. Men dropped before him, pushed back before his berserk madness. Foley swung the wrench down on Silvestro's head, but he had not been able to get in a good blow in the press around him. The wrench glanced off the back of Big Harry's head.

The foreman staggered for a moment, shook his head to clear it, as a wounded beast might do, then lunged through the crowd. They clung to him, trying to trip him, slugging at him with fists. For a moment it seemed that they would bring him down in spite of his flailing arms.

But the hot molten metal oozing along the floor bit at the feet of some of the men. They shrieked with pain, and leaped out of the way of the flowing rivers of steel. The others turned, startled, and in that moment Big Harry with a shriek of ungovernable rage lunged through the crowd, straight across the shop. Men who barred his way were hurled aside like tenpins. Silvestro reached the door, lunged out into the darkness of the night.

The shop workers followed him, racing after him into the open, intent on catching the murderer. Mike Foley was in the lead, still brandishing his wrench. But Harry Silvestro ran with such speed that he outdistanced them all. He raced down the wide street between the two long rows of shops, which stretched from Keystone's railroad station straight across to the Keystone River. Behind him the long line of pursuers stretched out, racing to catch him.

SILVESTRO WAS not fleeing haphazardly. With all the sudden madness that had abruptly seized him, there seemed to be a sureness in the flight, as if he knew just where he wanted to go. The whole of the mill district was thrown into an uproar by the chase. Men along the street took up the pursuit as they heard the shouts of Foley and the men from the Number Three shop.

They clung to Silvestro's trail through the night, followed him across the railroad sidings, close to the Keystone River, and saw him leap down the embankment toward the mud flats.

These mud flats, the dumping ground of the city, were the homes of hundreds of derelicts who each year converged upon the town of Keystone from the surrounding country. The human flotsam and jetsam gathered in the hovels along the river bank, and when they became sorely pressed for food, would take an occasional odd job in town or in the mills. Many of these men, wanted by the police of other cities, did not leave their mud flat homes at all, hiding until the search for them had cooled. This vicious conglomeration of derelicts and criminals had been tolerated in Keystone for a long time, with Mayor Richard Gaylord generally too busy to plan a concerted drive to clean up the town.

The town itself had been created by the Keystone Steel and Iron Corporation, and had been built up around its huge plant. Richard Gaylord, being one of the directors of the company, had been chosen mayor, and had served for five terms, consec-utively. In addition to his position with the Keystone Steel and Iron Corporation, Gaylord had extensive interest in the stock market, and commuted often between Keystone and New York as well as Chicago, which was near by. Since these derelicts in the mud flats had always been careful not to bring themselves to the attention of the authorities, no campaign had ever been started to drive them out.

Now, however, as Big Harry Silvestro raced toward the mud flats, these inhabitants of the town's underworld gave concrete evidence that they were a potential danger.

Silvestro had crossed the railroad siding which ran along the river, and was racing out toward the hovels on the flats, with the angry mob of workmen from the mills at his heels. Shouts and cries of rage filled the night, and many townsmen across the river in the residential district stopped to stare over, not knowing what was the trouble.

The workmen began to gain on Silvestro, and a lynching appeared imminent, for despite his great strength he could never have defended himself against the several hundred outraged workers in pursuit. But at that crucial moment that the hovels along the river's edge spewed forth their grimy, filthy, vicious occupants.

These derelicts and criminals raced out across the flats toward the approaching workmen, as if according to a well-laid plan. They were armed with automatic pistols, and there was a significant silence among them as opposed to the angry shouts from the workmen.

Big Harry Silvestro saw the aid that was coming to him, and stopped running, dropped flat on the ground. Almost at once a sharp command rang out among the criminals. The men raised their automatics, and streams of fiery flame lanced out through the night at the pursuing mill hands. Bullets whined through the air, and men screamed, dropped, mortally wounded.

The criminals continued to send volley after volley into the close-packed ranks of the workmen, and the mill hands were suddenly seized with panic. Cries of fright and terror rose from the press that had advanced with shouts of rage.

Fully thirty of them had fallen to the first volley, and as the automatics continued to spit their messages of death. More and more men fell, writhing on the ground, or lying still in death. The mill hands turned to flee in sudden panic, and the criminals, moving up at a second sharp order from among them, continued to fire until their guns were empty.

The cold-blooded slaughter kept up until the surviving mill hands had fled back across the railroad siding, leaving almost a hundred of their number dead or wounded along the mud flats.

To the startled watchers from the residential section across the river the shadowy figures of these murderous criminals appeared like horrid ghouls of the night. And the slaughter that had just taken place seemed incredible, fantastic, like some weird nightmare of the imagination. That such a thing as this could have taken place in the staid mill town of Keystone was beyond their comprehension. They watched, stunned, too amazed to take action.

And over on the mud flats a tall, fair-haired man whose left cheek was disfigured by an ugly scar was issuing further orders to the criminals. At his command, those desperadoes spread out over the flats, walking among the wounded mill hands. Whenever they found one who was only wounded, they would stoop and fire another shot into his brain. They left not a single one of those workmen alive. They moved about leisurely, not seeming to hurry, as if they had no fear of retaliation or capture by the police.

Big Harry Silvestro had arisen from the ground where he had thrown himself, and was now standing, watching the slaughter apathetically, with a dazed expression on his bovine countenance.

At last the fair-haired man with the scar uttered another sharp order, and the criminals left off their murderous search. The scarred man turned and made his way north along the river bank, with Silvestro close behind him and the other criminals following. They streamed toward the North end of the city, where a number of low class barrooms catered to the undesirable element in Keystone. The night swallowed them up, and there was no longer any sign of life along the mud flats.

The mill hands began to steal back, kneeling beside their dead comrades. Cries of rage and sorrow filled the night as they discovered friends and relatives among the dead.

A few moments later, almost the entire police force of Keystone came swarming across the Broad Street Bridge. They had been summoned from every portion of the city, by radio. But they were too late. The fair-haired man with the scar, Harry Silvestro, and all those criminals had completely vanished.

The police scoured the city, searching through every corner of the barrooms in the North End section, every room and cellar in the dilapidated tenements and boarding houses. The mill hands helped them with a will. But no trace of the criminals was found.

11

THE SPIDER

THAT NIGHT the town of Keystone went into mourning. Throughout the South End section where the poor but clean homes of the mill workers were located, there was weeping and lamentation. Close to five thousand families lived here in company-owned buildings. In a hundred of those buildings red-eyed women and sobbing children sat beside the biers of loved husbands and fathers who had been massacred that day.

On the other side of the river, in the better class residential section where dwelt the executives and supervisors of the Keystone Steel and Iron Company, there was perplexity and consternation. Over their breakfast tables the following morning this one topic was gravely discussed. It was dreadful that a man like Silvestro should suddenly go mad in this fashion; but it was beyond comprehension that the denizens of the mud flats should suddenly arise, fully armed, as if prepared in advance to protect Big Harry from the consequences of his deed.

Mrs. Silvestro and her four children were brought down to headquarters and questioned and cross-questioned for hours. The big mill foreman's wife had fallen into a state of acute hysteria upon learning what her husband had done. She could not believe that he had thrown Jack Markos into the bucket of molten steel. She screamed again and again: "No, no! Harry no do that! Harry he like Jack Markos—he like him very much. He no kill Markos. I no believe that!"

Investigators combed the mills and the homes of the workers, trying to get some clue, some inkling of the sudden malady which had seized Silvestro. It was clear from the stories of the workmen in the Number Three shop that Big Harry had appar-

12

ently been seized by some sort of cramp immediately before he threw Markos into the bucket. This was about all the investigators could get. Beyond that they were met by a stolid silence from the mill hands as well as from their families.

Mayor Richard Gaylord went into conference with Jonathan Spencer, General Manager of all the company plants in Keystone. But the crowning mystery of the whole terrible occurrence remained unsolved. That was the disappearance of the fair-haired man and his followers. There was absolutely no trace of them.

The city was beginning to quiet down a bit the following night, when disaster struck once more. A man in shop Number Four and another in shop Number Six suddenly broke into murderous action during the night shift, just as Silvestro had done the night before.

Kovalko, a furnace man in Number Four shop, drew a knife which he had had concealed in his belt, and slashed three men before he was overpowered. One of the men died, the other two were taken to the Keystone General Hospital across the river for treatment.

Strahl, foreman in Number Six, attempted to hurl one of his men into an open hearth furnace, but was prevented in the nick of time. He put up a furious resistance, when the other men leaped upon him, and, in the course of the fight, someone brought a sledge hammer down on the back of his head, crushing in his skull.

Kovalko, captured alive and taken to the city jail, hanged himself with his necktie before morning.

Now the town was truly aroused. It became evident that Big Harry Silvestro's act had not been an isolated case. Both Kovalko and Strahl apparently had been seized with the same kind of cramp from which Silvestro had suffered.

The next night another man went berserk, and the night after that, two more.

On the fifth night, police guards were placed in every shop, armed with clubs and sawed-off shotguns. On that night all of the men working in open hearth shop Number Three, where Big Harry Silvestro had been foreman, were suddenly seized with the same attack of cramps.

The fifty men began to mill around wildly, their eyes growing red with madness. They shouted, screamed, attacked and clawed at each other, and ripped open the vents which held the molten steel within the open hearth.

The police guards, summoned from all the other shops, subdued these men with their clubs, but had to kill three before they could quell the mad riot. The others were handcuffed and taken to the Keystone General Hospital for observation.

And there Dr. Arvin MacLeod, the Coroner of Keystone County, discovered the terrible truth. He phoned Mayor Gaylord hastily from the Morgue Room in the basement of the hospital, where he had finished the autopsy on the bodies of Kovalko and Strahl.

"Look here, Gaylord!" Dr. MacLeod's voice was fairly quivering with excitement. "It's a disease! The blood of Kovalko and Strahl is tainted with some foreign substance. I can't tell yet what it is. But I injected a drop of blood from each of them into some mice. The mice reacted just as the men did. But whatever it is that they have in the blood, the mice couldn't fight it the way the men did. They died within twenty minutes. I'm afraid it's some sort of epidemic, Gaylord."

Unfortunately, there were two newspaper reporters in Mayor Gaylord's office when he received the telephone call from Dr. MacLeod. MacLeod's voice, loud and agitated, was plainly audible to the reporters, and they heard every word of what he said. An hour later, every newspaper in the land had issued an extra carrying arresting big black headlines:

EPIDEMIC SWEEPS KEYSTONE!
SPREAD OF MURDER MADNESS
CAUSES STEEL TOWN PANIC!

CHAPTER 2
ENTER—THE SPIDER!

GAYLORD'S DAUGHTER, Susan, and her fiancé, young Charlie Hendrix, were also in Gaylord's office when he received the message from Dr. Arvin MacLeod. Susan Gaylord was a dark-eyed, dark-haired, pretty slip of a girl whose sweetness was heightened by the warm curve of her young lips. Charlie Hendrix was young, handsome, boyish. He had starred on the basketball and track teams at Harvard, would have made the football team but for lack of weight. His father was Crawford Hendrix, senior partner of Hendrix, MacIntyre & Hendrix, one of the largest stock brokerage firms of the country, with offices in New York, Chicago and two dozen other cities.

Richard Gaylord carried one of his stock accounts with Hendrix, MacIntyre & Hendrix, and it was through this connection that young Charley Hendrix had met Susan. The two young people had been strongly attracted to each other, and their engagement had followed as a matter of course.

Susan Gaylord and Charlie Hendrix heard every word of Dr. MacLeod's report over the telephone, just as the two reporters heard it. Gaylord frowned at the reporters, who scurried from the room to phone in their news story, but he made no attempt to stop them.

While Susan and Charley remained in the room, staring at him with wide eyes, Mayor Gaylord said into the phone: "Good God, MacLeod, do you know what you're saying? Do you mean to tell me that this homicidal madness is going to spread to everybody in Keystone? It'll mean we'll have to shut down our plant—"

"It'll mean more than that, Gaylord," Dr. MacLeod's dry voice informed him. "It means that the whole town will have to be quarantined. We don't know the nature of this disease, but it seems to be communicable. It means that you'll have to phone the Governor and ask him to assign state troopers—perhaps militia—to block off the town, and permit not a soul to leave. We're cursed with this plague, whatever it is, and we don't know how far it may spread if we don't bottle it up. Until we isolate the germ of this disease, we can't take a chance on its spreading outside the city."

Gaylord's knuckles grew white, as his hand tautened on the receiver. "But MacLeod, it can't be as serious as all that. Why, it's unheard of; a thing like madness can't be catching—"

"Apparently it is," MacLeod told him dryly. "The twenty-odd men who were brought here from the riot in the Number Three shop last night are all suffering from the same thing. They're the very men who chased Silvestro to the river bank. They saw their own friends and relatives slaughtered by those wharf rats. They're the same ones who saw Jack Markos, the timekeeper, thrown into the vat of molten steel. And yet, they've all succumbed to the same thing themselves. I'm sorry, Gaylord, but as County Coroner it is my duty to demand that you communicate with the Governor at once, and see to it that the town is sealed up!"

Gaylord hung up, and faced his daughter and her fiancé, with his shoulders sagging despairingly.

"You—heard?" he asked in a thin voice.

They both nodded. Susan Gaylord exclaimed: "Father! I can't—bring myself to believe that all these things are true. It—it seems like some terrible nightmare; the story of how Markos was thrown into the vat of steel, of how the mill hands were slaughtered on the river bank, and of how Silvestro and those criminals disappeared in the night, together with that man with the scarred face. Oh, father, I'm—afraid!"

Gaylord reached over the desk and patted her hand. Young Charley Hendrix came over and took her in his arms, and she rested her head on his shoulder.

Mayor Gaylord sighed. "I guess MacLeod is right. I'll have

to phone the Governor. I'll close all the shops, shut down the plant until this thing is solved!"

THAT AFTERNOON, two hundred and fifty state troopers were thrown in a wide cordon around the town of Keystone. They were armed with carbines and clubs, and their instructions were that nobody at all was to be permitted to leave the city. Keystone was officially placed under quarantine.

The entire plant of the Keystone Steel & Iron Corporation was shut down. The town was suddenly quiet as the blast furnaces ceased to thrust their flaring flames up into the sky, and the multitudinous noises of the rolling mills and the huge steel presses died into silence. The steel town of Keystone became quiet as the grave by comparison with the cacophony of noise which had overhung it before.

But the disorders did not cease. The mill hands were now stricken by real panic. Word had spread of Dr. MacLeod's findings, and men stared at each other suspiciously while womenfolk stayed within their homes, keeping their children off the streets. Fifty more cases of madness were reported during the day, and

RICHARD WENTWORTH

in many instances the afflicted men did much damage before they were finally subdued and removed to the hospital ward.

The state troopers did not enter the town, but merely guarded all the exits. The enforcement of law and order was left to the police force, of which Mayor Gaylord was himself the honorary chief. There was no official Chief of Police in Keystone, and Gaylord himself administered the department.

Many of the wealthier families attempted to leave town, but they were halted by the state troopers, turned back. Ugly murmurs began to arise in the mill districts. Agitators were circulating among the workers, urging them to attempt to break through the lines of state police and escape from the danger of being afflicted with that dreadful madness.

Gaylord sent every available policeman out on duty, ordering them to patrol in twos and threes for greater protection, and to quell any disturbances with an iron hand. He didn't want to be compelled to ask the Governor to declare martial law in the town. The Keystone Steel & Iron Corporation regarded this town as its own private property, and desired to set no precedents whereby the State Government might step in to supersede them.

It was that evening, in Mayor Gaylord's deserted office in the City Hall Building, that Charley Hendrix finally made the suggestion which was to bring the Spider to Keystone.

Gaylord had spent a long day, what with conferences with Jonathan Spencer, the General Manager of the mill, and with long distance telephone calls to New York and other cities, as well as to the Governor of the State. Jonathan Spencer was now in the Mayor's office, at the close of the day, arguing heatedly

with Gaylord, while Susan and Charley listened. Spencer had just finished
an explosive outburst in protestation
against the closing down of the mills.

"See here, Gaylord, do you know how
much we stand to lose by closing down?
We're working on a thirty-million-dol-
lar order for the new cruisers that the
Government is laying down. If we don't
get that steel out in time, our contract is forfeited. Don't you
realize what that means? I insist on opening the mills at once!"

Gaylord, usually the first to agree to any course of procedure
that would be profitable for the Keystone Steel & Iron Corporation, remained firm this time. His fist came down on the desk
with a hard thud.

"No, Spencer. As long as I'm in charge of the administrative
branch of this city, those mills won't open. We're not going to
risk contaminating the whole population. And we're not going
to risk any more riots in the shop. The Government will have to
give us an extension of time—"

"They won't give us any extension," Spencer growled. "We'll
lose the contract, and it'll go to the Smithtown Steel Company,
at the other end of the state. Why, this thing has already done
us enough damage. Do you know that our stock has dropped
ten points during the day?"

"I'm sorry, Spencer," Gaylord said firmly, "but the price of our
stock is not as important as the lives of men and women. The
mills remain closed!"

21

"We'll see about that," Jonathan Spencer roared. "I'm going to wire all the directors to call a special meeting. This is all bosh and bother about epidemics. MacLeod is crazy. This is all a plot of some sort, to close us up so that we lose the contract. Those men have probably been paid to act insane. And you, Gaylord, should be the last to fall for it. My God, man, you own a good block of Keystone yourself. You'll be ruined if the bottom drops out of the stock."

"Never mind about me," Mayor Gaylord snapped. "I'll take care of myself. And I'll also take care of the women and children of this city. You don't seem to realize, Spencer, that we owe a duty to those people. We owe them the duty of keeping them safe and healthy, and of protecting them against things like this. How could you ever sleep nights if you reopened the shop and hundreds of other men died as the result? I don't dispute your statement that there must be some plot afoot; the fact that those criminals from the mud flats were all armed indicates it. And from the reports of that fair haired man with the scar, I judge that they had good leadership. But that doesn't change the situation. We won't re-open the mills!"

Jonathan Spencer pursed his thin lips, and scowled. "We'll see, Gaylord, we'll see," he murmured softly. And he swung about, stormed out of the room.

MAYOR GAYLORD watched him leave, then shrugged and looked up at Susan and Charley.

"You two youngsters better run along home," he said. "Stay indoors. There may be more disturbances tonight. I should have

Big Harry swung a vicious blow that caught Mayor Gaylord in the face.

23

sent you out of town before the state police established their cordon around the city. But I was so busy, it slipped my mind."

Charley Hendrix took an eager step forward. "I have a suggestion, Mr. Gaylord. Susan has been telling me about the time, three years ago, when that racketeer from Chicago moved into Keystone and terrorized the city."

"I remember it," Gaylord said shortly. "What has that got to do with this trouble?"

"Nothing at all, sir, except that Susan tells me that at that time the city was saved by a mysterious person whose identity nobody knows—"

"You remember, father," Susan broke in. "It was the Spider. He was an awfully ugly-looking man, and he wore a long cape and a wide hat, and I was frightened by him at first. But it was he who finally saved the city."

Gaylord frowned. "That's true, Susan. The Spider did us a good turn then. But don't forget that the Spider worked outside the law. He's a hunted man himself. I don't think that I, as Mayor of Keystone, could ethically call upon him for help."

Young Charley Hendrix exclaimed impatiently: "But that's just what we need, Mr. Gaylord. The police seem to be helpless. They can't discover a single clue, they don't know where to start. A man like the Spider could go into the underworld and really accomplish things. With the lives of so many inhabitants of this city at stake, you can't let your official position stop you."

Gaylord frowned thoughtfully. "No, Charley, I don't think—"

"But you must, sir!" Charley Hendrix's firm young chin was thrust out at a stubborn angle. "I insist that you do it. You may do as you like with me, but if you don't send for the Spider, I will!"

Mayor Gaylord studied the young man for a long moment. "You *are* a chip off the old block, aren't you, Charley? Crawford Hendrix would talk just the same way. I believe you'd go ahead with your intentions even though it meant losing Susan, wouldn't you?"

Charley Hendrix hesitated.

Susan exclaimed: "He's right, dad. And I love him for being like that. When he makes up his mind to a thing, he always goes through with it—just like his father."

Mayor Gaylord threw up his hands in surrender. "All right, you win. But how can we send for the Spider! We don't know how to get in touch with him—"

"I think I know how to do that," Charley Hendrix told him. "There have been some disturbances in New York recently, and it is a matter of common knowledge that the city was saved from being thrown into the hands of a vicious criminal, only by the activity of the Spider. He apparently acted almost entirely on the side of the law in New York, and it is currently rumored that he is a close friend of Commissioner Kirkpatrick. Suppose you phone Kirkpatrick. Suggest to him that this is a case in which the Spider might be interested. And then see what happens."

Gaylord glanced at his wrist-watch. "Eleven thirty," he remarked. "I'd have to try Kirkpatrick at his home."

He picked up the receiver slowly, got long distance, and put through a request for a call with Stanley Kirkpatrick, Commissioner of the New York City Police Department. In less than five minutes he had his connection, and Susan Gaylord and Charley Hendrix listened eagerly while the Mayor explained the situation.

Kirkpatrick's voice over the phone held a serious note. "I've seen about it in the papers, Mayor Gaylord, and you have my earnest sympathy. If there is anything I can do, please feel free to call on me. Have you anything in particular in mind?"

"Yes, Kirkpatrick. It has been suggested to me that there is a certain person who is best equipped to handle a situation like this. Perhaps you know of whom I am thinking."

There was a significant pause at the other end. Then: "You mean—"

"I mean the Spider."

"Why do you mention the name to me?"

"We need the Spider here, Kirkpatrick. If there is any way that we can get in touch with him, beg him to give us his assistances—"

"I'd like to help you, Gaylord, but what makes you think that I have access to the Spider?"

"Nothing, nothing," Gaylord said hastily. "But if you should have the opportunity of communicating with him, I wish you would tell him that we need him."

"I'll bear it in mind, Mr. Gaylord," Kirkpatrick replied. "Perhaps the opportunity will arise."

They were fencing with each other, Gaylord eager to emphasize the need for the Spider, Kirkpatrick wary of committing himself.

Gaylord said: "The situation is much worse than you can guess, Kirkpatrick. If the Spider—"

He broke off as the sudden shattering of glass drowned out his voice. He raised his eyes, and uttered a shout of surprise. A huge fist had smashed through the window in the opposite wall. And now that fist smashed again and again at the jagged pieces of broken glass in the window pane, clearing the opening. Susan uttered a shriek, and Charley Hendrix swung around, amazed.

A terrifying figure appeared in the window, threw one leg over then the other, and vaulted into the room. The man was naked to the waist, with a square, brutish face and a close-cropped shock of black hair. His lips were drawn back from his teeth in a vicious snarl. He stood in a half crouch, glaring at the three.

Gaylord gripped the phone tight, and his lips uttered the words: "Big Harry!"

THE MAN who had broken into the room was Big Harry Silvestro, the fugitive foreman of Number Three open hearth shop.

Silvestro's red-rimmed eyes moved from Gaylord to Charley Hendrix, then settled on Susan Gaylord. He began to advance slowly toward her, his long, prehensile arms reaching out for the shrinking girl. Susan uttered shriek after shriek, and backed away, her eyes fixed on the huge, brutish man in terrified fascination.

Charley Hendrix shouted: "Get away from her, you!" He reached frantically into his back pocket, brought out a small revolver.

But before he could raise it, Big Harry Silvestro uttered a

27

growl of rage, swung around, and smashed a huge fist into Charley's face. Charley Hendrix was sent flying backward, to crumple in a heap in the corner, the revolver dropping from his nerveless fingers. He tried to get up, but slumped back, shaking his head, and groping on the floor for the gun.

Big Harry paid the boy no more attention, nor did he look at Gaylord. But he made straight for Susan, reached out and caught her by the shoulder just as she was turning to flee. Susan kicked, clawed and scratched, but Big Harry only laughed, raising her off her feet as if she had been but a paper doll. He swung her over his shoulder, and turned back toward the window.

Mayor Gaylord sprang up from his desk, raced around to stop him. "My daughter! Susan!" he shouted, and threw himself in Silvestro's path.

Big Harry only laughed again, swung his left arm in a vicious backhanded blow that caught Mayor Gaylord full in the face, sent him staggering backward helplessly. Big Harry dashed for the window, with Susan's screams ringing in his ears, and with Susan's little nails clawing at his naked back, digging deep furrows in his skin. But Silvestro did not seem to mind, or even to feel those nails. He threw a leg over the window-sill, just as Charley Hendrix succeeded in picking up his revolver.

Charley's nose was bleeding from the blow that Silvestro had landed, but he managed to raise the gun, aiming it carefully. He was afraid of hitting Susan, so he sighted low for Big Harry's legs. As he was about to pull the trigger, Mayor Gaylord scrambled to his feet, shouting with rage, and leaped toward Big

Harry, moving directly in the line of fire. As Charley Hendrix held his finger from the trigger, Gaylord leaped at Silvestro.

Big Harry kicked back with his right foot, caught Gaylord in the stomach and sent him crashing back. In a moment he had leaped over the window and disappeared with Susan.

The two men floundered after him, Gaylord sickened by the force of the blow at his stomach, and Charley Hendrix still dazed. They could hear Susan's screams dying into the night, but when they reached the window there was no one in sight. Big Harry Silvestro had disappeared with Susan Gaylord.

On the desk lay the telephone instrument which Gaylord had dropped. He staggered back toward the desk, gasping: "They've got Susan! Charley, they've got Susan!"

He was about to reach for the phone again, when Charley Hendrix exclaimed: "Look at this, sir!"

He was picking up a slip of paper from the floor. Gaylord straightened with an effort, holding his hand at his stomach, and stepped over to read the paper over Charley's shoulder. It was printed crudely in pencil, and it read as follows:

MISTER MAYOR—WE HAVE YOUR DAUGHTER, AND YOU KNOW HOW MUCH A LIFE MEANS TO US. YOU BETTER DO WHAT WE WANT, OR SUSAN TAKES THE RAP. YOU LAY OFF CALLING THE GOVERNOR. NO MARSHALL LAW IN THIS TOWN. ALSO, YOU LAY OFF CALLING FOR HELP FROM OUTSIDE. NO PRIVATE DETECTIVES, NO SPECIAL INVESTIGATORS. YOU'RE TAKING ORDERS FROM

US NOW, UNLESS YOU WOULD LIKE TO HAVE
YOUR DAUGHTER'S NOSE DELIVERED TO YOU
ALL WRAPPED UP IN A NICE BLOODY PIECE OF
PAPER. HAVE YOU EVER SEEN A PRETTY GIRL
WITH HER NOSE CUT OFF? SHE ISN'T PRETTY
ANY MORE.

There was no signature to the note, but a curious, rough drawing was appended at the bottom. It was a picture of a fool's scep-
ter with the curved staff ending in an upright portion that was
capped with the face of a clown or jester of the fifteenth century.
It was the typical staff which the king's jesters of medieval times
had been accustomed to carry; with this difference—that the
face of the jester was far from a foolish or silly one. The picture
had been drawn with great skill and cunning, and the face was
replete with evil. The mouth of the clown seemed to have been
slit across into the cheeks, and the face was a gargoyle of ugliness.

There was only that fool's bauble to serve as a signature. But
it was revolting enough, and even more terrifying because of the
fact that no name was signed to the note.

Charley Hendrix turned and looked with dawning terror at
the Mayor. "Mr. Gaylord! Only a madman could have written
this. We must save Susan!"

Gaylord laughed harshly. "That fool's bauble explained a good
deal. The man who wrote it wants to show us that he is dealing
with madmen, with fools, with idiots. That Harry Silvestro—
he was a quiet, hard-working man. Look at him now!" Weakly,
Mayor Gaylord staggered toward the desk. "No detectives, no
investigators. That means no Spider."

He picked up the phone, said: "Hello, Kirkpatrick. Are you there yet?"

"Yes, yes, man. What's happened? What's been going on there?"

Gaylord hesitated, glanced across at Charley Hendrix. Charley Hendrix leaned over the desk, whispered: "For God's sake, tell him never mind. We dare not send for the Spider now!"

Gaylord nodded, then forced a laugh. "It was nothing, Kirkpatrick. Say, don't bother about the Spider. I've—changed my mind. We don't want him here. You understand?"

"I think I understand," Kirkpatrick's voice came slowly over the phone. "Say nothing more about it, old man. If I can be of help in the future, call me."

Gaylord said: "Thank you," and hung up. His shoulders sagged helplessly as he stared across the desk at Charley Hendrix. "We'll—have to toe the mark, Charley, until we get Susan back."

WHEN RICHARD GAYLORD, the mayor of Keystone, hung up the telephone in his room, the click of the instrument travelled over a thousand miles of telephone line to the office of Stanley Kirkpatrick, Commissioner of Police of the City of New York. Kirkpatrick hung up his instrument, and stared solemnly across his desk at the faultlessly attired man who sat facing him.

This man had sat silently throughout Kirkpatrick's conversation with Gaylord. His attitude and bearing bespoke poise, culture, and great physical as well as mental powers. Throughout the telephone conversation he had maintained a well-bred air of disinterest while Kirkpatrick was talking to Gaylord. The deep-set, keen blue eyes were everywhere except upon Kirkpatrick, and he seemed to have no concern with what the Commissioner was saying.

When Kirkpatrick hung up, the visitor lit a cigarette nonchalantly. Kirkpatrick said: "This will interest you, Dick."

The visitor raised his eyebrows. "Interest me?"

Kirkpatrick grinned sourly. He said with elaborate sarcasm: "I beg your pardon, Mr. Richard Wentworth, sportsman and adventurer. Of course, the well-known Mr. Richard Wentworth wouldn't be interested in ordinary police matters, would he?"

Wentworth returned his smile. "Why not, Kirk? Everything in this exciting life of ours interests me. I heard you mention the Spider on the phone—couldn't help hearing it, old chap. Was it something in connection with the Spider?"

"It's about that business over at the Keystone Mills, Dick. That was Mayor Gaylord of Keystone on the wire. He called up to ask me to get in touch with the Spider for him. He said he wanted the Spider to come to Keystone." Kirkpatrick threw his visitor a queer glance. "Peculiar, isn't it, that he should think I could get in touch with the Spider?"

Wentworth shrugged indifferently. "Can you?"

"What do you think, Dick?" Kirkpatrick asked softly.

"Well, I don't know," Wentworth told him carefully. "The consensus of opinion seems to be that you have some sort of connection with the Spider. I wouldn't be surprised if the Spider is a good friend of yours."

"If he is," Kirkpatrick replied, "I'd be doing him a good turn by sending him to Keystone. I think he'd find the excitement that he seems to crave. Mayor Gaylord had just finished asking me to get in touch with the Spider, when suddenly there seemed to be some sort of interruption at the other end. He must have dropped the receiver for awhile, and when he came back on the line, his mood had changed entirely. He doesn't want the Spider any more. In fact, he asked me to forget all about his request."

Richard Wentworth seemed to be lost in deep abstraction. "Now that's queer, isn't it, Kirk? I wonder what could have happened to change his mind that fast?"

"I think," Kirkpatrick said very slowly, his eyes fixed upon Wentworth, "that the Spider would do well to go out to Keystone anyway."

Wentworth arose from his chair, and picked his hat, cane and gloves off the Commissioner's desk. "No doubt you're right," he said casually. Then he added as if it were an afterthought: "Oh, by the way, Kirk, I forgot to mention it before. I am leaving on a little trip today. Probably be away for a week or two. So don't look for me at the club."

Kirkpatrick restrained a smile. "Rather sudden, isn't it?" he asked drily. "Have you decided where you're going?"

"Oh, I thought I'd take a little trip out—er—out west. Just look around the country, so to speak."

"Out west, eh? Not going in the direction of Keystone, by any chance?"

"Keystone? Oh, yes, that's the town you just mentioned, isn't it? Well, I'll leave Keystone to the Spider. Good-bye, Kirk. I'll be seeing you in a couple of weeks."

He extended his hand, and the Commissioner grasped it warmly. "Good-bye, Dick—and be careful."

Wentworth hesitated for a moment as if he had something else to say. Kirkpatrick looked at him quizzically.

"You have something else on your mind, Dick?"

"Er—yes, Kirk. It is about Nita Van Sloan.* She'll be wanting to know where I have gone. Of course, if she should ask you, you don't know, do you?"

Kirkpatrick smiled. "Well, you haven't really told me where you are going, have you?"

Wentworth returned his smile. "You see, Kirk, I'd hate to have anything happen to Nita. When she hears I have left she will, no doubt, be around trying to wheedle out of you some information as to where I can be found. I'd hate to have you making guesses—"

"Such as—Keystone?"

Wentworth's poker face betrayed nothing.

Kirkpatrick laughed good-humoredly, clapped a hand on his visitor's shoulder. "Don't worry, Dick. I'll do my best to say nothing if she should come here. But you know Nita. It's hard to resist her."

"Well, Kirk, do your best."

Kirkpatrick watched Richard Wentworth's broad back through the doorway. As the door closed behind his visitor, a

---

* AUTHOR'S NOTE: Nita Van Sloan, whom Wentworth mentions here, will appear later in the story, where her relation to Wentworth will be more fully explained. To the readers of these chronicles she is no stranger, and those who have met her before will understand Richard Wentworth's love for her.

smile of warm friendship lit the Commissioner's face. "The best of luck to you—Spider!" he said almost in a whisper.

Between those two men there was a rare friendship—also an unspoken secret. If Commissioner Stanley Kirkpatrick suspected that his friend, Richard Wentworth, was in reality the Spider, he never uttered that suspicion. For it would mean that he would have to place his friend under arrest.

As Police Commissioner of the City of New York, he was sworn to uphold the law; and it was a matter of common knowledge that the mysterious being who was known as the Spider flagrantly flaunted the law in his unconventional campaign against crime. There had been many instances when the two blazing guns of the Spider had laid low a criminal whom the law could never reach. Nevertheless, Kirkpatrick was pledged to bend every energy to arrest and prosecute the Spider.

What he would do if he were ever confronted with the definite proof that Richard Wentworth and the Spider were one and the same man, Stanley Kirkpatrick dreaded to say. But be was morally certain that the Spider would be in Keystone within twenty-four hours....

CHAPTER 3
"YOU BET WE'LL FIGHT!"

THE SOUTH road leading into Keystone was barricaded.

The state police had erected a barbed-wire fence across the highway with a movable portion in the center which could be slid to one side to allow the passage of a single car at a time if necessary. But no cars were being permitted to leave or to enter the town. Troopers were on guard at this gate, as well as at similar points on all other roads leading into the town. Keystone was virtually under quarantine with a cordon of state police thrown all around it.

All shipping on the Keystone River was at a standstill. The sluggish waters of the river, running close alongside the south road, were not barricaded, but a trooper with a sawed-off shotgun stood at the edge of the road where he could command the river. A number of cars were pulled up in the road outside the barricade, and newspaper reporters as well as many curious persons who had come from the neighboring countryside were peering through the gate.

The troopers were constantly on the alert, each carrying a carbine. Several attempts had already been made by the panicstricken inhabitants to rush the gate and get out of this town in which an epidemic of madness seemed to be spreading. Twice the troopers had been forced to fire over the heads of hysterical mobs. The troopers themselves were careful to keep the townspeople at a respectful distance. They had seen the effect of the epidemic on people who had been stricken, and they had no wish to be caught by the dreadful malady.

At intervals, the sound of shooting and mob fighting had come to them from the heart of the city. They knew that matters were coming to a crisis in Keystone, and they were prepared for trouble.

The crowd in the road outside the barricade parted to make

way for a small coupé that approached slowly from
the south. The coupé stopped at the barricade, and
the driver slid from behind the wheel, just as the
sergeant in charge of the state troopers came toward
him, frowning.

The man leaving the coupé was tall, athlet-
ically built, with broad shoulders and trim waist.
He appeared to be in his early fifties, with graying hair at the
temples, and subtle lines of weariness around the mouth. If
Stanley Kirkpatrick, Police Commissioner of New York, had
been here at this moment, not even he would have recognized in
this middle-aged, dignified person the Richard Wentworth who
had been in his office on the previous day. Careful make-up had
removed every characteristic of personality from Wentworth's
face. Cunning patches of gray hair at the temples, the judicious
use of pigment and facial cream had transformed Wentworth's
appearance.

The crowd at the gate watched while the sergeant said gruffly:
"You can't come in here. The town is under quarantine. Turn
that car around—"

He stopped as Wentworth raised a hand. "I am aware of the
fact that Keystone is under quarantine. Nevertheless, I wish to
enter." Wentworth extracted a card case from his pocket, and
handed the trooper a card. The card, which had been printed
only last night, read: *Dr. Elias Benson.*

"I am a diagnostician," said the bogus Dr. Elias Benson. "I
have come here to study this disease which is scourging the city.
Your Mayor Gaylord has no doubt given you instructions—"

BAYER.

RICHARD
GAYLORD

CHARLEY
HENDRIX

"That's right," the sergeant said. He gave Wentworth a queer look. "It's your funeral, Doc. Go ahead. But I'll say you got plenty of guts, goin' in there."

Wentworth managed to look puzzled. "Guts?"

The sergeant nodded. "They had two diagnosticians here this week. Both of them went mad. They got caught by the disease themselves." He extended a hand. "My name is Murphy. Sergeant Jerome Murphy. I want to shake hands with you, Doctor. You're a braver man than I am. I'd never go in that town of my own free will!"

Wentworth smiled, accepted the trooper's hand. "A physician must never consider such things. However, I appreciate the compliment, Sergeant. And now, if you will open the gate—"

"Sure thing, Doc."

Wentworth got back into the car, and the Sergeant gave the word to his men. The gate was swung open, and Richard Wentworth, alias Dr. Elias Benson, alias the Spider, drove through the barricade and down the steep hill into the town of Keystone. He had worked fast since last night. He had created the personality of Dr. Benson, and wired to Keystone in that name, and had secured Gaylord's permission to enter the city for an attempt to diagnose the disease which was spreading like wildfire in Keystone, and driving the inhabitants to homicidal mania.

AS HE drove down into the heart of the city, he could look to his left across the Keystone River and the mill district. He frowned as he saw that the blast furnaces were all working as usual, and that all the shops seemed to be in full operation.

HARRY SILVESTRO

ARVIN MACLEOD

SUSAN GAYLORD

39

He had heard that Mayor Gaylord had ordered the closing of the entire plant. The move had seemed a wise one, and Wentworth could not understand why the shops were once more reopened.

There were dozens of barges in the river, unloading iron ore, coal, oil and other supplies onto docks close to the railroad siding, on the opposite shore. Here and there a tugboat lay idle in the center of the stream. It was apparent to Wentworth that the mills could not long continue to function, for no new supplies were entering the town. These barges must have come in before the cordon of troopers was laid down.

At each of the small bridges spanning the river, he could see a city policeman on guard. The stores along Main Street were open for business, but the sidewalks were almost entirely deserted. On this side of the river, the inhabitants of the town were keeping close to their homes. Lights were appearing as Wentworth drove along, for night was rapidly descending over the valley.

Richard Wentworth drove down Main Street until he reached the corner of Broad. At his right was the handsome City Hall building, and beyond it, on the opposite side of the street, was the Keystone General Hospital where the victims of this strange disease were being treated. But Wentworth did not go either to the hospital or to the City Hall building. Instead, he turned left on Broad Street and drove over the bridge into the factory section.

The policeman on guard did not stop him. Apparently the man was merely there as a precaution against mob rioters passing over into the residential section.

Once across the bridge, the entire atmosphere of the town changed. Hoarse shouts rose into the night, and here and there Wentworth could see small groups of policemen disbursing crowds of workers with swinging night clubs. Stores were all closed here, and the windows boarded up.

The open hearth shops, where the greatest disorders had occurred, were in full operation. Here he noted barbed-wire fence that had been erected around the entire plant. A detail of private company police stood guard. Other policemen patrolled the streets around the plant, dispersing any groups which attempted to form.

At one corner a little further on, a crowd of workers and their wives stood around a soap box orator whose frenzied words reached Wentworth.

"I tell you, men and women, its suicide to stay in this town. Every mother's son of you will go mad eventually. There's a plague in this town. They're keeping us here because they want the shops worked. When it comes your turn to go on the next shift, you'll go in those shops, and some of you will be stricken. Why should you go in there and take that chance for the measly pay that the company gives you? Stay out, I tell you. What if the company loses its contract with the Government? What do we care? Should we lay down our lives so that the company can fulfill its contract? I say no!"

Wentworth did not stop, but drove on past the open hearth shops, then made a right turn.

He knew this town almost as well as did the residents. Some years ago he had been here and had done a signal service to

the city. The mill workers all knew that
the Spider had saved them from a serious menace at that time. And though
they also knew the Spider was outside
the law, Wentworth felt he could still
command their respect and confidence.
He was going to put that feeling of his
to the test tonight.

HE STOPPED the coupé before a two-story building which
directly faced a vacant lot on the opposite side of the street.
Across that lot could be seen the barbed-wire fence around the
company plant, as well as the gate at which the police stood
guard.

Wentworth's glance travelled across to the building. The
ground floor was dark. The second story was brilliantly lit. A
plate-glass window extended across its entire width. Light
streamed through this window, illuminating the lettering upon
the glass, which read as follows:

STEEL WORKERS INTERNATIONAL UNION

Down below, in the lower left hand corner was the additional
wording:

MICHAEL FOLEY, PRES.

Wentworth nodded in satisfaction. He could see men moving
about up there in the lighted rooms. He had come at an oppor-
tune time. A meeting of the Steel Workers Union was in progress for some reason. Having acquainted himself thoroughly

42

with all the events that had taken place in Keystone since the beginning of this terror, he knew that Mike Foley was the crane operator who had been in the same shop with Harry Silvestro. He knew Foley very well, knew that the man had been thoroughly honest when he had last met him; also that Foley wielded great influence with the field workers not only due to his position as president of the local union, but also because of his personality, and his reputation for integrity.

Men were hurrying through the streets toward the entrance of the union building. Apparently the meeting was either in progress or about to open.

Wentworth knelt down on the floor board before the front seat, and took a small, flat leather case from his pocket. He opened this, revealing a mirror in the cupboard. Within the case itself rested tubes of pigments and facial cream, as well as small aluminum plates for changing the shape of the nose, and other accessories for use in disguise.

Wentworth rested the mirror of the case against the back of the seat, and proceeded to make swift use of the pigment. His nimble fingers moved over his own face with the skill and accuracy of an artist. Slowly the features of Dr. Elias Benson disappeared, giving place to a sallow complexion, discolored teeth, and lined, ugly cheeks. The face that finally peered back out of Wentworth's mirror was a face which was known and feared throughout the underworld of America—the face of that mysterious, as yet unidentified person who was known as the Spider.

Satisfied with his work, Wentworth closed the make-up case and replaced it in his pocket. Then he got out of the car, went around to the luggage compartment, and opened it with his key. Within this compartment was a large packing case that almost filled it. The cover of the case was off, and a casual observer would have been startled to see that it was full to the top with blued-steel automatic pistols and with boxes of cartridges.

Wentworth drew from a recess of the compartment, a long cape and a black hat. He locked the luggage compartment once more, threw his own hat in the car, and donned the cape and hat. The tall, athletic figure of Dr. Elias Benson had disappeared. A twisted, stooping figure crouched in the night alongside the car. This was the figure of the Spider. Many criminals had looked at that twisted shape, and had screamed their terror aloud. For where the Spider walked his misshapen way, criminals died.

That mysterious figure moved slowly across the street, almost blending with the night. No spot of color showed, not even the white face under that broad-brimmed hat. Black melted with night, and hurrying men were unaware that the Spider was passing.

THE SPIDER crossed the street, faded into an alley alongside the union building. He moved sure-footedly, soundlessly, toward the rear, and found the narrow side entrance which he knew to be there. The door was locked, but a moment's manipulation with a set of passkeys opened it, and the Spider faded into the corridor within.

He climbed the narrow, rickety stairs to the upper floor. Ordinarily, those stairs creaked and groaned when anyone ascended them. But the Spider made no sound. At the top, he found himself on a small landing before a thin, wooden door. The door was unlocked, and he silently twisted the knob, opened it a fraction of an inch.

This was the huge union meeting room. It was illuminated brightly, and the Spider could see rows and rows of chairs upon which sat the steel workers. They were facing this small door, which was at the left of the speaker's platform. Peering through the crack, the Spider saw the platform, with Mike Foley standing at the speaker's table and addressing the gathering. Behind Foley were seated four other men, apparently also officials of the union. Foley's voice was powerful, and carried ringingly through every corner of the auditorium. It was plainly audible to the man behind the door.

"Men," Foley was saying, "you all know the purpose of this meeting. Certain members of the union have demanded that we call a general strike until the epidemic of madness in this city is wiped out. Our men are dying not only from the epidemic, but they have been massacred in cold blood by a small army of murderers that are holed up somewhere in town. Every day more of our men go mad in the shops. Every day there are new attacks upon us. Only this afternoon that gang of murderers appeared again, and shot down forty men and women on Fleet Street in the South End. We are told that we are being given full police protection; but we are being slaughtered just the same. And we are unarmed, unable to defend ourselves.

"Men, I haven't got the slightest idea of what is happening. I don't know who it is that's driving our men mad, and I don't know who it is that controls this band of thugs that comes out every night to slaughter us. But I do say that we're not going to stand for it any longer!"

Foley's voice was almost drowned by the enthusiastic shouts of the hundreds of men who were packed into the meeting room. "You said it, Foley! We won't stand for it. We want to get out of this town. Close the plant! Stop work!"

These and a hundred other sentiments were expressed vociferously, at the top of their lungs, by the assembled men.

Foley raised his hand for silence, and gradually the shouting died down.

"Men," he went on, "if the five thousand workers in the steel mills of this city were to march out of town, the troopers would never be able to stop us. We have a right to protect ourselves. We have a right to get out of a place like this. We—"

Once more his voice was drowned by the shouts of acclamation. He waited until they were through shouting, then continued to talk.

"Before we take a vote, men, it's only fair that we should listen to the other side of the story. For that reason, I have invited Mr. Jonathan Spencer, the General Manager of the Keystone Steel & Iron Corporation, to come here tonight and speak to you. Let him give you his side of the story. Then we'll take a vote."

The Spider crouched silently behind the door while Mike Foley motioned to one of the men seated on the platform behind him. Jonathan Spencer arose. He was attired in a frock coat, and his bow tie was carefully tied. He bowed coldly to Mike Foley, then stepped forward to the speaker's desk, glared out over the heads of the audience.

THE MEN in the room began to heckle him, shouting: "It's old Money-mad himself. He don't care if we die or not. He wants his mills to work. Don't listen to him!"

Other men in the audience cried out: "Give him a chance. Let him talk. We'll hear his side of the story, anyway!"

Spencer stood there, tall and uncompromising, until the noise and the shouting had died down. A slight sneer of contempt twisted his lips out of shape.

"You men are all fools!" he began. "Don't you see that there is a conspiracy afoot to put our company out of business? These hoodlums who have been slaughtering you, and this epidemic that is spreading through the city, are all part of a deep-laid plot. Are you going to let yourselves be licked? Are you going to let yourselves be driven out of a job by a bunch of hoodlums led by a canny criminal? We are quarantined here in the city. As long as you must stay, why not work? I am sharing your risk and your perils. I'm in the plant every day, and I don't ask any man to take a risk that I won't take myself. We're working on a huge contract for the Government—"

He was interrupted by jeering shouts from the audience. "That's right, it's his contract. His contract is all he cares about. To hell with him. Let's give him the bum's rush!"

Chairs toppled over in the auditorium as the great body of men arose almost with concerted action, and began to rush toward the platform. Spencer had always been disliked as a hard task-master. Now the spleen of the working men was being given a chance to express itself.

Mike Foley shouted: "Stop! Stand back! Give him a chance—"

Foley's voice was drowned by the excited shouts of the aroused workers. They began clambering up on the platform, and clutching, grimy hands reached for Spencer. The General Manager stepped backward involuntarily, his face blanching at the raw hatred which he saw in the faces of the men who were attacking him. In a moment those men would have their hands on Spencer, and there was no telling what they would do to him in their present state of mind.

Foley tried to stop them, but he was thrust aside as if he had been a child. Men mounted to the platform, while Spencer backed away, reaching for one of the vacant chairs with which to protect himself.

And suddenly a strange, blood-curdling sound echoed through the room—a sound that caused all those men to stand as if petrified. It was the sound of a man's laughter; but such weird hilarity as might have been expressed by some robust god of the pagans upon viewing the antics of the silly little human beings upon this earth. It was laughter that reached into the marrow of men's bones, and froze it.

Involuntarily, all eyes swung toward the little door alongside the platform, from which the strange laughter had come. That door was now swinging wide open, and in the entrance stood the twisted, ugly, caped figure of a man whom many of them recalled having seen once before.

An awed whisper went up from those men in the room. "The Spider! It's the Spider!"

Slowly, Jonathan Spencer put down the chair which he had raised to defend himself with. Slowly, the rage died in the faces of the steel workers, and they backed quietly down from the platform.

Mike Foley exclaimed under his breath: "Thank God!"

The Spider's weird laughter ceased as suddenly as it had begun. And now, as the echoes of his hilarity died away among the rafters, the place grew suddenly quiet—except for the labored, excited breathing of the close-packed mass of men who watched him tautly.

THE SPIDER'S glowing eyes under the low-turned brim of his hat seemed to be everywhere at once. His cape bellowed out behind him as he leaped lithely up to the platform, and stood half-turned so as to face the audience though he did not expose his back to Spencer, Foley, or any of the other seated men. His voice rang with a note of steely authority.

"Men of Keystone! Many of you remember me. It seems that I have come in time to save you from an act of folly. Jonathan Spencer is right. Everything that has happened here points to a plot against the steel company. By calling a general strike, you are playing into the hands of the plotters. You must not do that. You must fight back."

A man in the audience laughed harshly. "That ain't the Spider; that's just one of Spencer's detectives dressed up to look like him. They figure we'll listen to the Spider. But they can't put that over on us—"

The man paused, as the Spider raised a hand. "I expected you would doubt my identity. I will prove to you who I am!"

He motioned with his hand. "Mike Foley! Come here. Come close to me."

Foley glanced hesitantly at the massed men in the auditorium, then at Jonathan Spencer and the other speakers on the platform. He shrugged, then advanced until he was standing close to the Spider. He gazed deep into the glowing eyes of the caped man.

The Spider's voice dropped so low that only the union president could hear. "You remember when the Spider was here last?"

Foley nodded wordlessly.

"Is there a way that you could identify the Spider again?"

Foley gulped. "Yes," he said. "There is a way."

"What is it?"

Foley grinned knowingly. "*You* tell *me.*"

The Spider nodded, apparently satisfied. "You remember when I shot the two men who were trying to knife you down at the waterfront?"

"I do."

"You remember the mark I placed upon their foreheads?"

"Yes. It was a little seal. Then we both left the building, to escape the fire. Those two bodies were burned, charred to cinders. That mark was never discovered on their foreheads."

"If you saw that mark again would you recall it?"

"I would."

"Then stretch out your hand, palm down," the Spider ordered.

Foley complied.

The Spider's hands moved so nimbly that it was difficult for any one of those who were watching them closely to see exactly what he did. From his pocket he had extracted a small cigarette lighter. He slipped open the bottom of this, pressed it against the back of Foley's outstretched hand, then with a motion so swift that it defied the eye, he returned the cigarette lighter to his pocket.

Foley was left there, staring with mouth agape at the small, blood-red replica of a spider which had been imprinted on the back of his hand.

"That—that's the mark of the Spider! That's the mark you left on those men's foreheads!"

"Now do you believe?" the Spider asked softly.

Foley nodded. "I—believe!"

He swung about, facing the audience of gaping steel workers. "Men!" he shouted. "This is really the Spider. I vouch for him."

There was a dull murmur among the men. They believed Foley implicitly. In addition, they had heard the Spider advocating a course of action directly contrary to that which Foley had advocated. If Foley identified the Spider, then it must be so.

The Spider stepped past Foley, and addressed the crowd in a strong, authoritative voice. "Foley has identified me. I think you men will admit that the Spider is your friend—"

It was apparent that the men in the audience took Foley's word. A subtle change had come over them. There were many places in the United States where the Spider would be shot at sight by the law enforcement officers if he were spotted. But in the town of Keystone, the Spider was known as a benefactor. Still, there were doubts in the minds of some of them.

The man who had interrupted now broke in again. "You want us to fight, Spider. What will we fight with? Gaylord won't even give us weapons. We can't fight those criminals with our bare hands—"

The Spider stopped him. "If you had weapons, friend," he asked slowly, "would you fight?"

"Would we! You bet we'd fight! Give us a chance at those guys—"

"Then you shall have weapons!" the Spider exclaimed. "Follow me!"

He swung around, took the amazed Jonathan Spencer by the arm, led him off the platform and out through the rear door.

CHAPTER 4
SILVESTRO FIGHTS

THE MEN all stared at one another in puzzlement, then Mike Foley shouted to them: "Let's go! What are we waiting for? The Spider is with us!"

With a shout they all trooped out after Mike Foley.

On the way down the stairs, the Spider was whispering to Jonathan Spencer. "Those men might have killed you, if I hadn't intervened. You were foolish to try to talk to them."

"But I had to keep the shops going!" Spencer told him fiercely. "The company has millions of dollars at stake. We can't afford to have them go on strike—"

"I don't agree with you," the Spider said coldly. "The lives of these men are more important than your company's contract. But at present it suits my purpose to have them continue to work for another day or so. Thus far, I have played into your hands,

Spencer. But I give you warning that when I order the men to leave your shop, *you are not to interfere!*"

They were outside now, and Spencer glared at his caped companion. "By God, Spider, your tone is too high-handed for me. I'll not close down the shops for any man!"

The Spider's hand gripped Spencer's arm so tightly that the General Manager winced. "You'll close them, Spencer—when I give the word. Now leave us. Get back to your office."

Spencer opened his mouth to speak, then seemed to think better of it, and turned away silently, hurried down the street without looking back.

The Spider crossed the street swiftly to his coupé, opened the luggage compartment once more, and waited for Foley and the steel workers to gather around him. Then he pointed at the packing case.

"Help yourselves, men," he told them. "There are your weapons!"

With exclamations of joy, Mike Foley and several of the men dragged the packing case out of the car onto the ground, and began to hand out automatics and ammunition.

The Spider watched them without a word. Back in New York the previous night, he had looted the warehouse of an exporting firm which was violating the Government Neutrality Act by shipping arms and ammunition to a warring country in Europe. These guns would be put to a far better use tonight than the exporters had originally intended for them.

The men busily loaded their guns, admiring them, commenting about them with the pleasure of children. Mike Foley came

"I show you!" he shouted as he brought the iron bar down in a crashing blow.

up to Wentworth, said: "Spider, we're taking orders from you. From now on, you're the boss—"

He got no further than that. His voice was lost in the sudden staccato racket of gunfire coming across the empty lot from the direction of the Keystone Steel Company plant. The sound of machine guns and pistol fire rolled through the night with startling abruptness.

The Spider was the first to sense what was happening. "The plant is being attacked!" he shouted. "Follow me, men!"

He swung about, and shot off at a long, easy lope across the empty lot. Mike Foley raced at his side, and the steel workers came after them, frantically jamming clips into their new automatics.

As the Spider came out into the street on the other side of the empty lot, he got a full view of what was happening at the gate in the barbed-wire fence around the company plant.

That same ugly crew of desperadoes, who had terrorized the city, slaughtering unarmed steel workers, were now attacking the guard at the gate. But now, instead of revolvers, they were using submachine guns. In the forefront of the criminals the Spider saw the huge, ungainly figure of Big Harry Silvestro. The desperadoes were firing with cold deadliness at the guard of patrolmen in front of the gate, which had just been opened to allow a truck to pass through.

Apparently the attack had been planned for just this moment. Half of the police were down, and the other half were returning the fire of the criminals desperately. The air was filled with the staccato barrage of the machine guns, mingled with the deep-throated roaring of heavy thirty-eights and forty-fives. The screams of men echoed above the gunfire.

THE SPIDER did not wait to see whether he was being followed by his men. He raced swiftly toward the scene of action, and his two hands crossed in front of his chest, came out each gripping one of his deadly automatics. His two guns began to spit fire while he was still running, and criminals wielding machine guns dropped before his uncannily accurate aim. Behind him Mike Foley began firing, as well as those of the other men who were in range.

The criminals were taken utterly by surprise. They had expected to be opposed only by the handful of guards at the gate, who would be mowed down by the first few blasts of machine-gun fire. Then, apparently, they had expected a clear entrance into the company's plant where they could work as much damage as they pleased.

With the sudden attack of the determined steel workers under the leadership of the Spider, they were thrown into confusion. These men were brave when the odds were in their favor. Now the odds were against them, and after half a dozen of them had dropped before the barrage from the Spider and his men, they uttered shrieks of terror and turned to flee into the night.

Big Harry Silvestro screamed at them, lashed at them with his fists to halt their panicky flight. But he could not prevail against their fear of bullets. In a moment the street was empty of desperadoes, except for those who had been felled by the new automatics of the steel workers. Big Harry turned, saw the advancing, menacing mass of workers, uttered a mad cry of rage, and leaped across the street, disappeared into an alley. The steel workers had hurried to the assistance of the police, and the Spider heard Mike Foley exclaim: "That's Big Harry Silvestro!"

The Spider shouted to Foley: "Take charge here. Place a man at the telephone in union headquarters, to await my orders. I'll be back!"

With those parting words, the Spider launched himself in pursuit of the fleeing Harry Silvestro. If he could capture Big Harry, there might be an opportunity for him to dig to the bottom of this conspiracy. He did not know whether Big Harry was acting under the influence of the disease which had stricken him, or whether he was a willing tool of the chief of this conspiracy. But whatever he was, he was a tangible lead, a possible avenue leading to the answer to a riddle of these massacres.

The Spider swung into the alley down which Silvestro had disappeared, and glimpsed the huge man's ungainly form twisting around a far corner. Wentworth sped after him, pursuing the man in silence. Silvestro glanced behind, saw the flowing cape and the wide hat, and seemed to be stricken with an excess of panic. He sprinted forward, swung around another corner; but the Spider kept doggedly at his heels, gaining upon him.

If Silvestro hoped to outdistance the Spider, he was doomed to disappointment. There were few racers who had ever been able to beat Richard Wentworth at intercollegiate track meets in Wentworth's college days. And throughout the years that followed those college days, Wentworth had kept himself in top form.

Silvestro was heading toward the river front. The pursuit

was carrying both men out through the mud flats. Wentworth could easily shoot Silvestro now, but he refrained. He wanted the man alive.

Silvestro reached the railroad siding. But instead of crossing into the dingy mud flats, he doubled back upon his own trail as if he had changed his mind, angling northward. They were in the open now, and Wentworth was gaining on Silvestro.

Big Harry stopped short, swung around suddenly, and raised his hand. He had a gun, and was pointing it directly at the Spider. His square, uncouth face was twisted into a hideous mask of rage as he fired three times in quick succession.

Wentworth zigzagged, still running toward Silvestro, with his cape billowing out behind him. In the darkness he was an uncertain mark. All three of Silvestro's slugs tugged at the Spider's cape, leaving three ragged holes. But the Spider was untouched.

His gun apparently empty, Silvestro uttered a scream of terror as he saw that the Spider was still unhurt. He drew back his arm, hurled the empty gun, but it went wide. The Spider continued to race toward his quarry. Big Harry, lost in panic, swung around, raced in a straight line across the railroad siding toward the mud flats.

THE CHASE pointed to the group of houses where the desperadoes had lived. The Spider made ready to draw his gun if assistance appeared for Silvestro. But there was no sign of life among the dilapidated shacks. They passed half a dozen of them, and then Silvestro ducked into one of them, no more than a one-room shanty with a sloping roof, where a dim light burned.

The Spider saw the shanty door slam shut, hurled his body

against the door, and sent it crashing inward. Ripping from its rickety hinges, it fell to one side. The Spider landed on hands and knees, blinked at the light of a guttering candle, and leaped lithely to his feet, just as Big Harry Silvestro rushed at him with both huge hands flailing.

Wentworth's face twisted into a grim smile. This was what he wanted. He could whip Silvestro into submission in a hand to hand fight; and he felt confident that if Silvestro were whipped, the man would talk.

He blocked Silvestro's blows with little difficulty, circling with superb footwork. Silvestro followed him, frantic with fury, seeking to land a single blow that would knock out his opponent.

But the Spider never was there for Silvestro's fist. Always that evasive figure danced out of reach or sidestepped, and each time Silvestro missed, his shadow landed a telling blow against the huge man's face. Each crash of the Spider's fist sounded like the dull blow of a sledgehammer on Silvestro's jaw, nose, or cheek-bone. Soon Big Harry's eyes were discolored; his lips were swollen and bleeding. As he fought, the Spider noted out of the corner of his eyes an open trapdoor in the far corner of the room. He sensed that Silvestro had been trying to maneuver him toward that open trap door, possibly with the intention of hurling him down into it. He deliberately allowed the man to work him over in that direction, then suddenly changed from defensive to offensive tactics. His two fists worked in and out with the deadly efficiency of piston rods, *smacking* with ruthless thoroughness against Silvestro's naked torso. The big man's abdomen became raw and red from the continuous blows, and he suddenly doubled over, unable to stand it.

The Spider stepped back, brought his right fist up in a short, hard uppercut to the side of Silvestro's jaw. It rocked the big man's head far back, sent him staggering just past the open trap door, to crash against the far wall. But with all the weight and power that the Spider had put behind that blow, he had failed to knock out Big Harry Silvestro. The bloody, begrimed shop foreman leaned against the wall.

Wentworth said: "Give up, Silvestro. You can't win."

Silvestro scowled, said through bleeding, cracked lips: "Vat you vant?"

"I want you to talk. Who made you like this? Who is the boss of these criminals?"

Silvestro snarled. "I no talk nodings!"

"All right," the Spider said regretfully. "I'll have to give you some more of the same."

He stepped in, and Silvestro, unable to back away, put up his fists automatically. Once more the Spider's hard blows thudded into Silvestro's stomach, and face. The big man was on the defensive now. He tried to cover up ineffectually. In spite of his great weight, in spite of the massive spread of frame and the rippling muscles of his body, he was no match for the Spider's skill. Once more a blow sent him reeling into a corner. He almost slid to the floor, with the whole room dancing before his eyes.

And the big man's hands, groping blindly on the floor, suddenly came in contact with cold metal. It was a crowbar, left on the floor by some workman. Silvestro's face assumed a guarded look of cunning as he felt the weight of the heavy bar.

The Spider was saying: "Well, Silvestro, are you ready to—"

With a yell of bestial rage, Silvestro raised the iron crowbar above his head, gripping it with both hands, and jerked to his feet, leaping across the room at the Spider.

"I show you!" he shouted, as he brought the iron bar down in a crashing blow toward the Spider's unprotected head.

In a fight, the Spider could act faster than the average man could think. He had so developed his mental processes and their coordination with the muscular system that the reaction from a brain impulse took place simultaneously with, instead of following, that impulse. A hard life of constant peril had brought this coordination of mind and muscle to the acme of perfection in the Spider. The automatic reaction of any man in his position would have been to draw a gun and shoot at the juggernaut of destruction that was leaping at him across the room in the shape of this huge giant wielding the deadly crowbar.

But the Spider wanted that man alive. He crouched, then threw himself in a low tackle that caught the leaping giant almost in mid-air, while the crowbar descended with a murderous thud upon the floor at the spot where the Spider had been. The impact of the Spider's shoulder against Silvestro's legs sent the giant tumbling to the floor, and the crowbar flew from his hand. Silvestro rolled over and over, toward the table near the wall, upon which stood the single candle that gave light in the room. Silvestro jack-knifed to his feet, and his huge arm swept across the table, hurling the candle to the floor. Its sputtering light was snuffed out.

The shack was plunged into darkness, and the Spider crouched, waiting tensely, his ears pitched to catch the slightest sound of motion. He heard Silvestro's labored breathing, heard the man's cautious footfalls on the floor, and prepared to tackle him in the darkness.

But instead of moving toward the door, Silvestro leaped suddenly toward the far corner of the room. In a flash the Spider understood what he was doing, and leaped after the man, but he was too late. Silvestro had jumped clear through the trapdoor.

From below came a sound of a dull thud as Silvestro's body landed.

WITH SWIFT fingers the Spider drew his flashlight, sent the beam of light stabbing down through the open trapdoor. He was just in time to glimpse the shambling figure of Silvestro leaping along a dark passageway at the bottom of a ten-foot drop. The Spider leaped down unhesitatingly, landed on hands and knees, then scrambled up, sent his light down the corridor in which he found himself.

This was a long passageway which had been cut into the ground underneath the shacks, and it ran east and west. The beam of light outlined Big Harry Silvestro racing around a curve in the passage, and the Spider dashed after him. Big Harry's footsteps echoed hollowly through the dark corridor, as they took one turn after another. The sides of this passageway were lined with rock, and the Spider noted that it had apparently been cut through the point of least resistance—that is, where the rock ended. This was the reason for the curves and twists in the corridor.

The Spider began to gain on Silvestro again, aided by the flashlight. Big Harry's footsteps sounded louder and louder, but he remained out of sight because of the turns in the passage. Suddenly, as if he had stepped into a void, the sound of Big Harry's footsteps ceased.

The Spider stopped short, listening carefully, but could hear no sound. Cautiously he advanced, throwing the light ahead of him, until he came to a point in the passageway where it forked. The Spider hesitated.

Big Harry had gone down one of these, but it was strange that his footsteps had ceased to echo. Cautiously, the Spider sent his flashlight flickering down the left hand passage, saw that it was lined with gravel, like the one in which he was standing. He swung his light to the right hand passage, and the answer to Big Harry's disappearing footsteps lay there before him.

The floor was a bed of oozing mud instead of gravel. Big Harry must have gone this way, the mud accounting for the sudden cessation of footfalls. The man's big footprints were clear.

The Spider had lost valuable time at the fork. He hurried through the right hand passage, his shoes *squishing* each time he took a step. He progressed more slowly now, for perhaps a hundred feet, until the passage began to rise in a sharp slope. He could hear the lapping of water, and in a moment he came out of the passage, to stand almost at the bottom of the slope of the mud flats, with the waters of the river not six inches below him. Big Harry Silvestro was not in sight.

The Spider clicked off his flashlight, so as not to make a mark of himself in the night for gunfire, and stood silently, listening for sounds. There were none, except the soft lapping of the water. Out in the middle of the river, several barges and a couple of company tugboats were anchored. Aside from that, there was no sign of life here. Big Harry Silvestro had disappeared as if into thin air.

For a moment the Spider let his gaze wander from one to another of the boats anchored in the river. There were two tugboats, and each of them carried riding lights. The barges were dark, deserted. The Spider clicked on his flashlight once more, let the beams play across the tugboats, and a hail came from one of them.

"Who's that with the light?" a jittery voice asked.

"I'm looking for someone," the Spider called back. "Did you see a man on shore here just now?"

"Not a soul, until you came along," the man on the tugboat replied. Then, with a note of suspicion: "What are *you* doing there? Who are you? Speak up!"

The Spider did not reply. He did not wish to indulge in lengthy explanations now. His flashlight had told him that the nearer of the two tugboats was called the *Miss Susan,* and the one further down the river, the *Miss Nettie.* Both were owned by the Keystone Steel & Iron Corporation, as were the barges.

The man on the *Miss Susan* clicked on a powerful flashlight which he directed toward the shore. "I got a gun here!" he shouted. "You better speak up, or I'll shoot!"

The man's voice was nervous and high-pitched. He could not be blamed, considering the conditions in the city.

Wentworth quickly slipped back into the passageway, began to retrace his steps toward the shack. He had had Silvestro within his grasp, and had let him go. Now he must start all over again, to seek some clue, some answer to the weird events that were taking place here in Keystone. Grimly he retraced his route toward the shack....

CHAPTER 5
ABOARD THE "MISS SUSAN"

FOR SEVERAL minutes after the Spider had reentered the tunnel, there was utter silence along the shore and out in the river. Nothing stirred; even the dim, shadowy figure of the watchman on the Miss Susan was motionless.

Then a dark shape rose slowly out of the water, clinging to a rope that hung from the gunwale of the tugboat. Water glistened from the man's naked torso as he scrambled agilely up on the deck. The man with the searchlight went to the rail and helped him over.

A light went on in the cabin, and momentarily illuminated the face of the watchman. He was no ordinary tugboat employee. Fair-haired, with an ugly scar across his left cheek, anyone in Keystone would have recognized him as the leader of the vicious band of criminals in their assaults upon the steel workers.

He scowled at the dripping man who had climbed out of

the water, and said: "That was the Spider on the shore, wasn't it, Silvestro?"

Big Harry Silvestro loomed a head taller than the fair-haired man with the scar; but it was apparent that he feared him thoroughly. He spoke in a subdued voice, haltingly: "Yes, Gregory—"

The fair-haired man's open hand came up in a sharp slap to the side of Silvestro's face, rocking the big man's head. Big Harry cringed.

"Do not be so familiar," the fair-haired man said coldly. "You will call me Mr. Bayer."

"Yes, Mr. Bayer." Big Harry lowered his eyes before the other.

"That is better. Now, tell me what happened."

"The Spider, he see me at the shops, and he chase me. I knew you and the men be coming back here through dat shack, so I not go there. I lead Spider around in circle, to give you time to get on board boat, then I run to shack. I t'ink he no see me in the night, but that damn Spider, he too clever. You leave candle burning there, and he see the light, break in the door. We have big fight."

Gregory Bayer was watching Silvestro closely. "Yes? You fought? And you did not kill the Spider?"

Big Harry uttered an oath. "Me bigger man than him. Me strong man. But that damn Spider—he's a devil. I got big crowbar, see, but even that no good. I punch, he dance away. Then he smack me. Cut up my face, sock me in belly, till I almost can't get up no more. So I knock over candle and jump through trapdoor. Then I swim out here and hang on rope till he go away. We fooled him, no?" Big Harry grinned through split lips. Gregory

Bayer looked thoughtful. "I wonder if we did. That Spider is very clever; too clever. We will have to do something about him. We must not allow one man to spoil our plans."

He waved a hand. "Go to your quarters, Silvestro. Fix up that face of yours. It's badly damaged."

Silvestro started across the deck. "Wait till I meet that guy again. I smash in back of his head. He no know what hit him!"

Big Harry scrambled down the companionway into the hold. Here some seventy men were packed closely together, sleeping on mattresses on the floor. These were all that was left of the gang of desperadoes who had attacked the company plant that night, after slaughtering steel workers and their families during the week. Machine guns and automatic rifles were stacked in one corner of the hold.

These men, like Big Harry, wore queer, pinched expressions. Criminals they were; murderers they were. But there was something else about them—something that was almost inhuman—which set them apart from other men. That strange something was the look of bestial ferocity that glowed in their eyes. Looking at them thus closely in the smelly, crowded hold, one might have sworn that every vestige of human emotion had been removed from their souls—if they had any souls—by some mysterious process of chemistry or black magic

They paid no attention to Silvestro. Big Harry moved among them surlily, picked a spot on the floor, and plopped himself down. He felt gingerly of his face, and one of the criminals, seeing his battered features, guffawed loudly. Big Harry swung around, glared at the man, who subsided at once.

68

Big Harry grunted: "You laugh, huh?"

"No, no, Harry, not me!"

"Hah!" Silvestro lumbered to his feet, started toward the man. The fellow screeched, tried to scramble out of the hold. But Silvestro's huge foot lashed out, caught the man in the temple with a sickening thud, sent him crashing into a bulkhead where he slumped in a limp heap.

Big Harry turned away from the unconscious man, callously, and glowered around the hold. "Anybody else vant to make laughing at me?" he demanded truculently.

Nobody answered him....

ABOVE DECKS, Gregory Bayer had thoughtfully watched Big Harry's broad, naked back disappear down the companionway. Then he turned and stared for a long time out over the river toward the shore where the Spider had stood at the mouth of the underground passage. The ugly scar on his cheek glowed redly in the darkness.

From a sheath under his coat he drew a thin, silver-like knife, with a bone handle. He hefted the vicious weapon in his hand, then ran the keen edge along his thumbnail. A chuckle sounded far down in his throat. With a swift motion he *swished* upward through the air, holding the knife like a sword. It was a practice thrust. Had an antagonist stood before him, that thrust would have disemboweled the man.

Again Gregory Bayer chuckled, replaced the knife and walked quickly across the deck toward the cabin. This was no ordinary tugboat. On the bridge, the wheel was lashed, but a seaman stood guard, and saluted smartly as Bayer passed him, stepped into the chart room. The chart room was equipped as no tugboat had ever been equipped before. There were maps, and a multitude of instruments, such as might have been found upon a seagoing yacht. It was apparent that this tubby craft could navigate the Great Lakes if necessary, in spite of its awkward appearance. In a rack on one wall of the chart room hung a row of the newest type of Browning rapid-fire machine guns, capable of firing a steel-jacketed bullet that could pierce armor-plate.

Two officers in the chart room saluted Bayer as he went through, and he returned the salute carelessly.

Within the cabin he seated himself at the desk, and reached for an open box of candy at his elbow. He ate half a dozen pieces of the confection, smacking his lips in evident enjoyment. It was strange to see this heavy-set, hard-faced man eating bonbons with such relish. Gregory Bayer had killed many men in the course of his career, and had not hesitated to inflict torture upon countless others. And always he had managed to have a box of candy near him.

He was a Russian. He had been a spy for the Russian Imperial Secret Police before the collapse of the Czar's government. Skillfully he had managed to ingratiate himself with Kerensky, then with the Soviets, and had risen to the position of Commissar. His ruthlessness and his cruelty had become a proverb. Finally the man's excesses of atavistic sadism had become too much for the government. An investigation revealed his past as a Czarist spy, and Gregory Bayer had been forced to flee. His knowledge of languages helped him to live on the Continent for a number of years, until he found the various capitals of Europe too hot for him. America was his next port of call. The craving for candy followed him.

He stuffed a large chocolate-covered cream into his mouth, and swung the swivel chair around to a sending and receiving radio set, built into the wall of the cabin. He fiddled with it for several moments, then spoke into the microphone.

"Number One. Number One. Number One. Number Two calling. Number Two calling Number One...."

He repeated the call several times, then waited, with ear-phones clamped to his head. At last he caught a reply. "Number One answering Number Two's call. Make your report quickly. I have little time to spare."

Gregory Bayer answered respectfully: "Our attack on the Company Plant was a total failure, sir. We failed to reach our objective due to interference from a well-armed body of steel workers under the leadership of the Spider."

"The Spider! You say the Spider is there?" Number One's voice grated through the ether, rasping into Bayer's ear-phones. "It's impossible. He couldn't have come so soon!"

"I'm sorry, sir," Bayer replied, "but I'm sure it was the Spider. No one else could have beaten Big Harry Silvestro in a rough-and-tumble fight. Even I couldn't do it—bare-handed. Silvestro's face is almost cut to ribbons. The Spider must have brought guns in with him, too, because all those steel workers were armed. My men weren't prepared for anything like that, and the steel workers shot down almost half of them. Mayor Gaylord must have sent for the Spider in spite of the warning note. What will we do with his daughter? Shall I have her nose cut off, as we threatened?"

Gregory Bayer's voice was as cool as if he were discussing the weather instead of proposing to cruelly disfigure a beautiful, innocent girl.

"No, no," Number One rasped. "Do not harm the girl unless I give the word. I am sure Gaylord wouldn't have sent for the Spider, knowing that his daughter is in our hands. The Spider must have come on his own. We need the girl, alive and healthy, to prevent Gaylord from asking the Governor to establish martial law."

"Then what'll I do next, sir?"

"You will leave Keystone at once, with all your men. We have no time to make another attempt at our objective here. The plan is too accurately timed to delay any longer. You will steam down the river to Croton City. Our operation at the Croton Steel Plant must begin tomorrow. I will personally take charge of the campaign in Keystone."

"But the State Police are guarding the river and the road—"

"You must pass them, Bayer. It is imperative that you and your men be in Croton City by tomorrow. How you do it is your concern. You understand, Bayer—" the voice coming over the ether became silky, dangerous—"what happens to a Number Two man who must be replaced?"

"I—understand, sir. I'll get through somehow, depend on it."

"As for the Gaylord girl, you will keep her on board with you. I think it best that she should be taken out of town, out of reach of this Spider. But remember that no harm must be done her. As long as she remains alive and in good health, we can depend upon it that Gaylord won't call on the Governor to declare martial law here in Keystone. You have your instructions. Communicate with me tomorrow, when you reach Croton City. Now sign off."

As Gregory Bayer removed the ear-phones and shut off the radio, there was a half-cunning, half savage smile on his thin lips. "So you're riding high, Number One! And Gregory Bayer is expected to lick your boots, eh? Well, what you don't know won't hurt you!"

Savagely he pressed a button, at the same time stuffing a couple of pieces of candy into his mouth. To the man who answered his call he ordered: "Bring that Gaylord girl in here—quick! And tell the first officer to get up steam. We're leaving at once—down the river for Croton City. Pass out the Brownings to the men below, and call me five minutes before we reach the State Police barricade."

The man saluted and left. In a moment he was back, leading Susan Gaylord.

The dark-haired, slender girl sank back against the wall, watching Gregory Bayer with half-frightened eyes. The man who had brought her in saluted, and left the cabin, closing the door softly behind him.

Gregory Bayer's eyes burned hotly as he let them wander in lascivious enjoyment over her slender body.

"You are very beautiful, Miss Gaylord," he said softly.

She made a visible effort to repress her fear of the man, and forced a smile. "Thank you," she replied. Her lower lip was trembling. "W-what are you going to do with me?"

"We are going out of town, my dear," Gregory Bayer told her. "I thought that perhaps you would provide a little entertainment for me on the trip."

Slowly he got up from his chair, his eyes still fixed on the girl. Susan Gaylord whispered: "No, no—" Gregory Bayer lunged at her, and she screamed, twisted out of the way. He swung after her, and his big hand reached out, gripped her dress. Hysterically she pulled away, and the dress tore in Bayer's hand. Susan screamed again, leaped toward the door, and tripped. She fell, her head striking the door jamb, and lay still.

Gregory Bayer stood over her, frowning. Under his feet the boat began to tremble as it got under way. They were moving down the river. Bayer scowled. He turned to the water cooler, seemed to change his mind, then shrugged and opened the door, stepped out of the cabin. He went up on deck, leaving Susan Gaylord to lie unconscious on the floor.

In the chart room, the first officer was passing out the Browning machine guns to the men, who had come up from the hold. They were spread out on the deck, along the rail, with the guns so placed as to be hidden from view of the bridge tenders along the river. As the boat progressed down stream, bridge after bridge opened for it without question. None of the bridge tenders entertained any suspicion of one of the company tugboats.

Gregory Bayer strode up and down along the deck, cautioning the men to silence.

"Well reach the State Police barricade in a half hour," he told them. "You will do nothing to attract attention. Don't shoot unless I give the word. If we can pass the state troopers without a fight, so much the better."

Silence descended upon the *Miss Susan* as she worked slowly down the river with her crew of desperate killers.

NEITHER GREGORY BAYER nor any of his men noticed the coupé which drove along Main Street, parallel with the river, slowly pacing their tugboat. That coupé contained two men. The face of one was shrouded by a broad-brimmed black hat, and he wore a long cape about his shoulders. He was driving. Beside him sat broad-shouldered, stubborn-jawed Mike Foley, president of the local Steel Workers' Union.

The Spider had not been entirely fooled by Silvestro's ruse. He had worked his way back through the passageway, into the shack where the fight with Silvestro had taken place. There he had stood for ten long minutes, watching the boats on the river. At last he had seen the *Miss Susan* get into motion. And the Spider had nodded his head in satisfaction. By a process of elimination he had deduced that the only place where Silvestro could have taken refuge was in one of the boats anchored in the river. The fact that the *Miss Susan* was getting into motion at this late hour of the night convinced him that his deductions had been correct.

Swiftly the Spider hurried off across the railroad tracks, retraced his steps past the company plant where ambulances were already picking up the dead and wounded to be transported to the Keystone General Hospital. He did not stop here, but made his way back to where he had left the parked coupé. The armed steel-workers were waiting outside the union headquarters, talking excitedly among themselves in groups. Mike Foley was waiting beside the car. When he saw the Spider he hurried over to him, smiling broadly.

"We put it over on them that time, Spider! That's the way to handle them all right!"

Wentworth gripped Foley's arm. "Quick, Foley! Give orders to your men to await us here. You're coming with me. Have somebody on the telephone all the time, in case we need them. There may be another fight within the next half hour!"

Foley's eyes glowed with excitement. He asked no questions, but immediately issued instructions to the gathered steel workers, and assigned two men to stay at the telephone at all times. Then he got into the car, and the Spider drove swiftly away, crossed the Broad Street Bridge long before the *Miss Susan* had reached it on its way down the river. They drove back up Broad Street until they came abreast of the *Miss Susan,* then turned around and paced it. Twice during the tugboat's progress, they crossed small bridges just ahead of it, and Foley leaned far out over the car to peer down upon the deck of the moving boat.

"I think you're right, Spider," he said eagerly. "It's kind of dark down there, but I think I can see a lot of men on the deck. What do you think they're up to?"

"They must be trying to get out of town. How far is the next city from here?"

"Croton City," Foley told him. "It's a steel town, a little bigger than Keystone. The Croton Steel Works are located there."

Slowly the Spider nodded. "I think I see the idea. We've got to stop them. This is the second phase of their plot. If they are not hamstrung now, this thing will spread to every steel town in the country. Whoever is behind it is playing for very big stakes, Foley."

The union president was tense with excitement. "Let's phone the boys, Spider. They can head this boat off before—"

"No. Not yet. As long as your steel workers confine themselves to the other side of the river for the protection of their homes and their women and children, nobody can have any quarrel with them. But if they should attack a company boat, that would be a different matter."

The Spider slowed his coupé down, allowed the tugboat to pass them in the river. Then he said to his companion: "Get back to union headquarters, Foley. Have the men ready to start at once. Commandeer as many cars as you can. I'm going to see Mayor Gaylord, and try to get him to deputize all of your men. I'll phone you from the Mayor's office, and if I put it over, you can start for the river to head off the tugboat."

"Okay," Foley said. He got out promptly, started across the bridge toward the mill district. The Spider swung the car around in another turn, and drove back toward City Hall. Before reaching City Hall, he turned into a dark side street, pulled the coupé up to the curb, and removed his hat and cape. A few moments' work with his make-up kit expunged the features of the Spider, replacing them with those of Dr. Elias Benson—the disguise which Wentworth had used upon entering Keystone.

He sat more sedately behind the wheel, and his every action was that of a dignified physician. He drove swiftly to Broad

Street, and parked before the City Hall building. Descending from the coupé, he made his way up the broad steps, finding his way easily to Mayor Gaylord's office. He had been in this very building, in the very office of the Mayor on his last appearance in Keystone.

He rapped upon the door, and entered when a voice within called out: "Come in."

CHAPTER 6
SLAUGHTER ON THE RIVER

WENTWORTH RECOGNIZED two of the four men in that room. On his last visit to Keystone he had met Mayor Gaylord. Jonathan Spencer he had seen only a little while before at the union headquarters. The other two men in the room were young Charley Hendrix and Dr. Arvin MacLeod.

All four men regarded him questioning. He stepped up to the desk, bowed in dignified manner, and placed a card on the glass top before Mayor Gaylord.

"Permit me to introduce myself, Mr. Mayor," he said. "I am Dr. Elias Benson from New York."

Gaylord raised his eyebrows. "Quite so. You phoned for permission to enter Keystone, Dr. Benson. I want you to meet Mr. Jonathan Spencer, the General Manager of the Keystone Steel & Iron Corporation, Dr. Arvin MacLeod, the Coroner of Keystone County, and Mr. Charley Hendrix, a close friend."

Wentworth shook hands in turn with each of the men. Although his appearance was entirely casual, his keen eyes were

79

NITA
VAN SLOAN

appraising every one of them. He could see that Mayor Gaylord was visibly under a great strain. The man's face was almost yellow in texture, his hair was disarranged, and his collar wilted. He had the appearance of not having slept for several days. Young

Charley Hendrix was also distraught, nervous, and manifestly at his wits end. Jonathan Spencer seemed to be in a towering rage about something. He glared at Wentworth as if the interruption were most unwelcome. There was no sign in his eyes to indicate that he recognized in the dignified Dr. Elias Benson the man who, only a short while ago, had saved him from the rage of the steel workers at union headquarters. He shook hands brusquely, and stamped away to the other end of the room, where he stood with his back to the others, looking out of the window.

Dr. Arvin MacLeod shook hands with Wentworth a little more cordially, but there was a slight trace of suspicion in his voice as he said: "I am extremely glad to meet you, Dr. Benson. I somehow recall having seen your photograph in the newspapers some years ago, but your appearance is quite different from the picture, as I remember it—"

"That was a number of years ago, Doctor," Wentworth said easily. "Perhaps you confuse the photograph with that of some-one else."

MacLeod shrugged. "Perhaps. However, my memory for faces is ordinarily very good."

The name of Dr. Elias Benson was a famous one among the diagnosticians of New York. Wentworth had assumed it to enable him to gain easy access to the city. He had deliberately taken the risk of meeting someone here who might know Dr. Benson. It was a risk that was absolutely necessary. He saw that MacLeod's suspicions were not entirely quieted, and welcomed the change of subject as Mayor Gaylord broke in.

"I want to tell you, Dr. Benson, how much I appreciate your coming here. It has been almost impossible to get anyone to enter the town since the epidemic of madness broke out. Even the state police won't come across their barricade. Luckily, the epidemic does not seem to be spreading very rapidly, although we have a few new cases every day—just enough to keep the quarantine strictly in force."

"From what I hear," Wentworth said, "this must be a very rare disease indeed. Have you progressed very far in your work of identifying it, Dr. MacLeod?"

"No, I'm sorry to say. I find some fine substance present in the blood of every individual who has been stricken, but there is no category within my knowledge of medicine into which that substance fits. I shall be glad to have you conduct any examination you care—"

"Thank you," Wentworth broke in. "Tomorrow I shall be glad to visit the hospital with you. Tonight, I think there is a matter of even greater importance, in which I am sure you will all be interested."

JONATHAN SPENCER did not turn from the window.

But Charley Hendrix took an eager step forward, while Gaylord pursed his lips.

Wentworth had wanted to approach the subject of the tugboat in a less abrupt manner, but time was precious. Soon the *Miss Susan* would be at the barricade, and once they passed the state police guard, the men could scatter from the boat without difficulty.

"I understand," he went on, "that Miss Gaylord was abducted—"

Charley Hendrix exclaimed: "Yes! She was taken right out of this room, from under our noses. We scoured the city, but there's not a trace of her!"

"Can you assign any reason for the abduction?" Wentworth asked.

"A very good reason," Gaylord told him bitterly. He opened the top drawer of his desk, extracted from it the note he had received, and handed it across to Wentworth. "There you are, Benson. I haven't given this note out to the newspapers. Only a few of us know about it. That's why I haven't asked the Governor to declare martial law here."

Wentworth read the note carefully, inspected the fool's bauble which was drawn at the bottom of the sheet of paper. The evil face of the jester, drawn with an uncanny ability, stared up at him with its ugly, slit mouth.

"If I could only get Susan back," Gaylord explained, "I could be my own man again. I dare not ask the governor for troops while Susan is in their hands!"

Dr. MacLeod said drily: "I doubt if you could get troops in

here anyway, Gaylord. The Governor wouldn't want the responsibility of sending the militia into a town with an unknown epidemic. Imagine what havoc would be wrought if the troops should be taken with the same kind of madness that seized Silvestro and the others!"

"What I can't understand," Charley Hendrix said, "is where they could have taken Susan. They must have some hideout in the city. They escaped after they slaughtered the steel workers at the river bank, and they escaped again after that attack on the company plant this evening. But there isn't a place in the city that hasn't been searched. They seem to have disappeared into thin air!"

"Not quite thin air," Wentworth told him. "Have you given thought to the idea that they might have made their headquarters on board one of the boats in the river?"

Jonathan Spencer swung around from the window where he had been standing, as if he had been stung by a bee. "That's ridiculous!" he exploded. "The only boats in the river, inside the city limits, are company-owned boats, and they're all in charge of trustworthy, reliable men.

"I don't know who you are, Dr. Benson, but I *will* say—" and he glanced significantly around the room, letting his gaze rest for a long minute on Charley Hendrix—"that we certainly have a lot of meddlers in this city now. First our friend Mr. Hendrix, then the Spider, and now you. For anyone to claim that a company boat is being used as headquarters for these criminals is absolute idiocy!"

"I'm sorry if I have given offense," Wentworth said mildly.

"However, it is possible that these desperadoes have overcome the crew of one of your boats. I did not mean to imply that the company had any part in this conspiracy."

Gaylord grunted. "Don't mind him, Benson. Spencer is just interested in one thing—keeping the shops going. And he doesn't care how many people die, or what happens to my daughter—" Gaylord's voice grew caustically bitter—"as long as he can fill his contract!"

Charley Hendrix was impatient. "You were talking about Susan, Dr. Benson. What about her? You think she's on one of those boats?"

"I do. Upon arriving in the city this evening, instead of coming directly here, I drove across one of the bridges into the mill district. I talked with many of the workers, including the president of the Steel Workers' Union. I wanted to get some first hand information on the symptoms of this epidemic of madness. On my way back, I happened to notice one of your company tugboats—the *Miss Susan*, if I'm not mistaken—steaming down the river. There were men with guns on the deck, and I am sure I saw a young woman on the bridge."

WENTWORTH WAS deliberately lying about having seen Susan on the tugboat. He was doing it in order to make sure that the *Miss Susan* would be stopped before reaching the barricade. He waited to see what reaction his words would have upon the four men in the room. Upon that reaction he would base his deductions as to the head of this conspiracy.

He entertained no delusions that this campaign of terror might be an abortive attempt on the part of some second-rate criminal. Thus far nothing had been stolen, no definite aim accomplished by the spread of the epidemic or by the attack against the steel workers and the company plant. There was something behind this campaign that was far deeper than the hope of immediate gain. And the person behind it must be a man of intellect, holding a high position in the city; otherwise it would have been impossible for him to lay the groundwork secretly for such a major operation.

Dr. MacLeod frowned. "You are sure of this, Benson? You're sure your eyes didn't deceive you in the night?"

Charley Hendrix was almost shouting in his excitement. "Let's stop that tugboat, Mr. Gaylord! Order the police after it. Phone the state troopers at the barricade. Quick, do something, for God's sake! That boat will be at the barricade soon!"

Gaylord seemed uncertain just what to do in this crisis. "Susan!" he murmured. "Susan, aboard that tug! And with all those criminals!" He groaned. "Why didn't we think of searching the boat before!"

Jonathan Spencer sneered. "I'm sure Dr. Benson must be mistaken. Why don't you send a couple of city patrolmen to stop the boat while it's still in the river? They can satisfy themselves that the boat is moving on a legitimate errand, and that there are no captives on board."

"Yes, yes," Gaylord said eagerly. "That's the thing to do. I'll have a couple of men go on board—"

"If I may be pardoned for intruding," Wentworth broke in, "I would suggest that it may be necessary to send more than just a couple of men. If this tugboat is really manned by the desperadoes who have massacred the inhabitants of this city, they will make short work of one or two patrolmen. You must concentrate as many men—"

"But I can't move them all at once, and leave the rest of the city unguarded," Gaylord protested.

"I have thought of that," Wentworth replied. "I notice that the steel workers across the river have all been armed. There must be more than a hundred of these armed men, ready and willing to fight. They've already beaten those criminals once, at the company's plant. Why don't you deputize them, and let them stop the tugboat?"

"I won't do it!" Gaylord exclaimed stubbornly. "Those men have no right to carry arms. Why, I'd be the laughing stock of the country if it became known that I deputized a gang of steel workers to attack one of their own company's tugboats."

"But what about your daughter?" Wentworth demanded. "How would you feel if your daughter should be carried out of town by Silvestro and those others?"

Jonathan Spencer barked: "Hah! You don't have to worry about that. The tugboat will never pass the police barricade."

Charley Hendrix was glancing from Gaylord to Spencer. Suddenly he pounded the desk with a frantic fist. "My God! Are you two going to sit there bandying words all evening while they're carrying Susan off? Why don't you do something? Aren't you going to do *anything?*"

Gaylord's voice sounded like that of a broken old man. "I'm afraid there's nothing we can do, Charley. If we send the steel workers against that tugboat, and if those desperadoes are really on the tugboat, a pitched battle will result. Susan may be killed. Our best bet is to let the state troopers stop the *Miss Susan.*"

"Of course," Dr. Arvin MacLeod broke in suavely, with a sharp glance at Wentworth, "this all depends on whether Dr. Benson here really saw what he says he saw."

Wentworth glanced sharply at MacLeod. He detected that same note of suspicion in the Coroner's voice that had been present when he mentioned the photograph in the newspaper. He shrugged, with an assumption of carelessness.

"Well, it's none of my business how you handle this situation. I'm a stranger in the city, and my only interest is a scientific one. However, I should think you would take some action about it, as young Mr. Hendrix here suggests."

Charley Hendrix gripped Wentworth's arm in desperation. "Look here, Dr. Benson, you seem to be the only sensible man here. Will you come with me? I'm going to try to stop that tugboat!"

"With pleasure," Wentworth told him.

The two of them hastened from the room, leaving Spencer, MacLeod and Gaylord staring after them.

OUTSIDE, WENTWORTH got into the coupé with Hendrix beside him, and drove swiftly down Main Street. He was reproaching himself bitterly now for having gone to see Gaylord at all. He should have ordered the steel workers to attack the tugboat without consulting the Mayor. It would have been a drastic thing to do, but the more he thought of it, the more he felt that he would have been justified in imperiling the lives of the steel workers in such an attack.

Even now he hesitated to call Mike Foley. If the tugboat were manned by the criminals, they could mow down the steel workers with their machine guns from behind the security of the deck rails. The steel men would not have a chance against them.

Wentworth had to drive almost to the edge of town before he caught sight of the *Miss Susan*. She was chugging slowly through the night, and was now less than twenty yards from the barricade. Wentworth raced his car down darkened Main Street, while Charley Hendrix urged him to more and more speed. But he was too far away to beat the tugboat to the barricade.

Ahead, he could see one of the state troopers step off the road to the edge of the river and raise his hand in signal to the tugboat to stop. The *Miss Susan* was almost abreast of the barricade on the road, but she gave no sign of slowing down.

Charley Hendrix shouted into Wentworth's ear: "You must have been right about that tugboat! Look, she's not even slowing down for the state troopers!"

Four or five other state troopers had run to the edge of the river, and they were all waving to the tugboat to stop. But there was no sign that anyone on the tug had seen or heard the troopers. She continued serenely on her way.

Wentworth could see Sergeant Murphy standing at the edge of the shore, could see the Sergeant draw the revolver from the holster at his side, and fire into the air across the tugboat bows.

Almost as if that had been a signal, red flames lanced out from machine guns all along the rail of the *Miss Susan*. The staccato bark of the deadly Brownings beat a terrible tattoo of death, riddling the bodies of the unfortunate troopers with steel-jacketed slugs. Sergeant Murphy and the other men on the edge of the river fell at the first volley, their bodies almost cut in half by the vicious barrage. Other state troopers rushed to the edge of the river, only to be met by a continuous hail of lead.

Wentworth drove furiously, recklessly, with Charley Hendrix hanging out of the window, peering ahead. Hendrix suddenly pointed at the tugboat, and screamed against the whistling wind: "There's Susan! There's Susan!"

They could see her clearly now, her torn dress flying behind her as she raced across the deck of the tugboat toward the rail. They did not know that she was half dazed from the blow she had sustained in the cabin. They did not know that she had regained consciousness only because of the rattling volleys from the machine guns. She was running, not knowing where she wanted to go, but half frantic with hysteria and fright. Behind her lumbered the burly figure of Gregory Bayer.

Susan reached the rail, tried to leap over into the water, but Bayer caught up with her, threw a thick forearm around her slender waist, and heaved her backward.

The Brownings were still chattering, sweeping the shore clear, beating again and again into the dead and wounded bodies of the unfortunate state troopers on the road. And the tugboat was slowly passing the barricade.

Wentworth brought his car to a halt with its nose touching the barbed-wire barricade across the road. He ripped open the door, leaped out, just as Charley Hendrix jumped out from the other side. The machine guns had stopped their rat-tat-tat, and Wentworth watched with bleak eyes while the *Miss Susan* moved unmolested down the river. Charley Hendrix pointed frantically.

"That big brute caught Susan! See him? He's dragging her into the cabin! God! What'll we do about it?"

There was no one here with them now, except for the lifeless bodies of the state troopers. Wentworth's mind was made up in a moment.

"The two of us can't stop that tug, Hendrix," he said swiftly. "But are you game to board her with me?"

"Board her?" Charley Hendrix asked blankly.

"Of course!" Wentworth snapped. "It's dark. There are no lights on the tub-boat deck. See that hawser dangling from the gunwale? We could swim out in the darkness and climb aboard, mingle with the other men. Quick, before she gets too far away from us. What do you say?"

Charley Hendrix looked at Wentworth with sudden suspicion. "Either you're crazy, or you're playing a trick to get me on board. Why, man, you could never get away with that! We'd be discovered in a minute. Our clothes would be dripping wet and they'd notice us. Who are you, anyway? Dr. MacLeod seemed to have some doubts about you."

Suddenly, Charley Hendrix placed both hands on Wentworth's arms, gripped them tightly, pressing them to Wentworth's side. "I think you're a fake! You're just posing as Dr. Benson. You're in with those criminals!"

From down the slope leading toward the city Wentworth could hear the sound of shouts and running feet. People were quickly coming to the scene of the shooting. If they were to go on board the *Miss Susan*, they must act at once. It was imperative to allay young Hendrix's doubts. He could see that the young man was wrought up, almost hysterical with worry about Susan Gaylord. He would have to trust Hendrix with his secret. He had been in town only a few hours, and he did not know whom to trust as yet. But he must take a chance with Hendrix.

SLOWLY, WITHOUT apparent effort, he twisted his arms out of Hendrix's powerful grasp. Young Hendrix strained against the pressure of Wentworth's arms, but it was no good. Wentworth twisted his arms slowly inward, then up and out, and Hendrix was forced to let go. Charley stepped back, with an expression of wonder in his eyes.

"Good God!" he exclaimed. "You're strong! I used to play basketball, and fence. I have strength in my wrists and my fingers; yet you broke my hold without trying. Who—are you?"

Wentworth stepped close to the young man, met his gaze squarely. "Were you in Gaylord's office when he phoned to Commissioner Kirkpatrick in New York?"

"Y-yes. I was there. Why—"

"That was when Susan Gaylord was kidnapped, wasn't it?"

"Yes. Why—"

"Gaylord was asking Commissioner Kirkpatrick to get in touch with a certain person, wasn't he?"

"Yes. How do you know—"

"I am that person!"

Charley Hendrix's jaw dropped open in amazement. "You— the Spider! I should have known—"

"Now—" Wentworth pursued his advantage—"will you follow me?"

"Yes, Spider—*anywhere!*"

Wentworth nodded, turned and raced back toward his coupé, with Hendrix behind him. He slid back the bolt of the gate in the barricade, swung it open, then leaped into the coupé. Hendrix joined him, Wentworth had the car started almost at once. He raced through the gate, sped down the road after the tugboat.

His eyes were glued to the *Miss Susan,* and he did not notice the small car which had been approaching the city, and which pulled over to the side of the road as he sped by. He, therefore, did not see the young woman who was driving that car, nor did he see what she did after he passed her. Had Wentworth seen that car and its occupant, the events of the next few days might have been materially altered. But whoever it is that directs the fate of men ordained that Wentworth should speed by without noticing either car or driver.

He raced down the road, with lights out, until he had gotten well past the tugboat. The men on the *Miss Susan* were paying little attention to what was occurring on shore. They had successfully passed the barricade, and that was all they cared about. Wentworth pulled the coupé up to the side of the road about a hundred yards beyond the tugboat. He leaped out, followed by Hendrix, and raced down the sloping side of the river bank, to the edge of the water. It was pitch dark here, and there was no chance of their being observed by the men on the boat.

The two of them waited tensely until the tug had come almost abreast of them in the middle of the stream, then Wentworth buttoned his coat tight about him, and plunged into the water in a clean dive that made no sound. Hendrix followed him, and the two of them swam silently toward the boat.

Sounds of shouting and wild jubilation came to them from the deck of the *Miss Susan*. Those desperadoes were celebrating their bloody victory over the state troopers. Gregory Bayer had disappeared into the cabin with Susan Gaylord. The watch on board was relaxed, and in the dead darkness no one noticed the two dripping figures that hoisted themselves over the side of the boat and swung on to the deck. Many of them were tilting bottles of liquor to their thick, bestial lips. Others were merely standing about or shouting with the mad joy of victory.

The figure of Big Harry Silvestro loomed above the others on the deck.

Silently, Wentworth and Hendrix stole across the deck, and ascended to the bridge. Their dripping clothes left a wet trail behind them. The man at the wheel glanced suspiciously at them, but said nothing.

Wentworth whispered to Hendrix: "Are you armed?"

Hendrix nodded. He produced a gun, and Wentworth said: "Okay. Let's go."

THEY ENTERED the chart room, where there was only a single man. This was the First Officer. He looked up, saw their dripping garments, and frowned, in puzzlement. He took a step toward them, and Wentworth came in at the man, brought up a smashing blow to his jaw. The First Officer crashed backward, uttering a shout of warning which was cut off as the back of his head struck a chair. The man collapsed in a limp heap on the floor, unconscious.

Outside, the man at the wheel turned to see what was the trouble, and Charley Hendrix covered him with the revolver. The door at the far end of the chart room, leading into the cabin, was suddenly swung open, and Gregory Bayer appeared.

He began to bellow: "What's happening—"

Then he saw Wentworth, and his hand went for the gun in his shoulder holster.

Wentworth's draw was a thing of miraculous swiftness. He had Bayer covered almost before the other's hand had touched his shoulder holster. Wentworth would have pulled the trigger without mercy at that moment, but just then Susan Gaylord leaped out of the cabin from behind Bayer.

She had seen Hendrix, and she ran across the cabin, directly in the line of fire. She was shouting: "Charley! Charley! I knew you'd come!"

That action of Susan Gaylord saved Gregory Bayer's life. The Russian stepped quickly into the cabin, and slammed the door.

Susan Gaylord had run across the cabin, and Charley Hendrix, forgetting everything, took her in his arms, trying to cover the patches where her torn dress showed her bare white skin. "Susan darling!" he said softly. "My dearest Susan!"

Wentworth scowled, then shrugged. These two young people were truly in love with each other.

The man at the wheel had seen what was happening in the cabin, and now he bawled out in a loud voice to the men on the deck below: "Quick, boys! The boat's attacked! Up there!"

Wentworth streaked out of the cabin like a thunderbolt, launched himself at the quartermaster. The man swung away from the wheel, brought up his hands to defend himself, but Wentworth forged through with scientifically pistoning fists. He landed two blows, smashing through the man's defense. One went to his stomach, the other to the side of the jaw, and the quartermaster dropped like a log. Wentworth swung away from him without even waiting for the man to hit the deck, and sprang to the companion ladder, up which half a dozen of the desperadoes were swarming, guns in hand.

Orange streaks of fire lanced through the night as the men shot at Wentworth. Wentworth's two guns sprang into his hands with the speed of legerdemain and his answering fire swept the attackers off the companion-ladder. Screams of agony from the wounded men who had been hurled to the deck below came up to them.

Wentworth sprang away from the head of the companion-ladder, called to Hendrix: "Over here, Charley. Hold this ladder for a minute!"

Wentworth raced back to the engine room signal box, and pressed the button marked "Stop." It would be a few minutes before the engineer below learned of what was happening above deck. In that time, he would still obey signals from the bridge. Almost at once the throbbing of the engines ceased as the engine room obeyed Wentworth's order.

Now, other men were swarming up the ladder, and Charley Hendrix was firing at them. Wentworth sprang to his assistance, slipping new clips into his automatic. In a moment his guns were blazing down at the attackers once more, and they fell away before the deadly fire.

Someone on the deck below shouted: "Let's jump! We can't stay on the boat!" Big Harry Silvestro, who stood out head and shoulders above the others, yelled: "To hell with dat!"

He snatched up one of the Browning machine guns, raised it to his shoulder, his finger on the trip. In a moment that machine gun would spray the bridge with deadly lead. Wentworth raised his left arm, rested his automatic on his forearm, took careful aim, and fired once. The slug caught Silvestro square in the forehead, sent the huge man hurtling backward, to trip over the rail and plunge into the river.

The death of Silvestro sent panic into the hearts of the other desperadoes. There was a concerted scramble for the rail, and they leaped over the side into the river as fast as they could. In almost no time the deck was deserted. From the engine room, the engineer and his crew of two men appeared on deck, saw what was happening, and likewise ran to the rail, leaped over.

Wentworth uttered a short laugh. These killers were all the same. They had no courage. They were brave only when faced with defenseless men or women. He swung around, leaped past Susan Gaylord, who had been standing on the bridge, leaning against the wall of the cabin, with both hands pressed hard against her breasts. Wentworth threw her an encouraging smile, then went through the chart room and tried the door of the cabin. It was locked.

"Better come out of there!" he shouted to Bayer. "The boat is taken. You might as well give up."

From outside came the sound of Susan Gaylord's shriek.

Wentworth twisted about, leaped out of the chart room onto the bridge in time to see Susan pointing at a dark figure which had emerged from the side window of the cabin, onto the bridge. It was Bayer. Bayer saw Wentworth, and jumped from the bridge, landing down on the deck on all fours.

Wentworth might have shot Bayer even as he crouched there on all fours, for he knew by now that the man was without conscience and without human instinct, an enemy of society and a peril to the city of Keystone while he was alive and at liberty. But he had emptied his automatic at the attackers coming up the companion-ladder, and his guns were useless for the moment. Bitterly he watched Bayer look up from the deck, then saw the Russian leap across to the rail, and dive into the river.

"That man should have been the first to die!" he said bitterly.

Later on, he was to realize only too well the truth of his words….

THE ENGINES were silent, and the tug-boat was drifting toward the west bank. Wentworth paid no attention to the drifting boat, but walked somberly around the side of the bridge, and climbed into the cabin through the window by which Bayer had escaped. He looked around, studying the room, and noted the radio set alongside the desk. A light was on and off just above it.

Wentworth stepped over to it, put on the ear phones and depressed the receiving key.

A voice rasped in his ears: "Number One calling Number Two. Number One calling Number Two. Number Two, why don't you answer? Number One calling Number Two!"

Wentworth's eyes glittered with sudden inspiration. He threw in the sending apparatus, spoke into the transmitter: "Number Two standing by. Number Two standing by."

The same rasping voice replied: "Number Two! Where have you been? I've been calling you for five minutes!"

"I'm sorry, Number One. I wasn't in the cabin—"

"You should have stood by for my messages! Have you passed the state police barricade yet?"

"We are past it."

"Good. Keep a sharp watch. You are suspected. A Dr. Benson, together with young Hendrix, are driving out to intercept you. So far, no armed force will attempt to attack the boat. Try to capture Benson and Hendrix without disturbance. Proceed at once to Croton City."

Wentworth asked cautiously: "Whom shall I get in touch with in Croton City?"

"Get in touch with? You will get in touch with no one. You know what you are to do. You will receive instructions from me by radio—"

Suddenly the rasping voice ceased for a moment, then went on with a note of suspicion. "What is the matter with you? Is this Number Two talking?"

Wentworth savagely clicked off the transmitter. "Compliments of the Spider, Number One. The boat is past the police barricade, but your men have fled from it. Your plans are slightly disarranged, I'm afraid. I don't know who you are yet, Number One, but you have the Spider's promise that you will die within twenty-four hours!"

Wentworth savagely clicked off the keys controlling the set, and ripped the ear phones from his head. If Number One had not been so keen, Wentworth might have had an opportunity to learn his identity.

For several minutes he paced up and down in the cabin, his mind racing over the situation. Only three men had known that he and Hendrix were going to intercept the *Miss Susan.* Those three were Mayor Gaylord, Jonathan Spencer and Dr. Arvin MacLeod. Number One must be one of those three.

Wait! Mike Foley had also known. But Foley had not known that Hendrix was going along. That should eliminate Foley, except that he might have spied upon Wentworth, watched him come out from the City Hall building with Hendrix. So Foley must still be included among the list of suspects. But he had definitely narrowed it down to those four men.

He tried to recall every movement, every word, every gesture that they had made during the time he had been in contact with them. Some slight thing that they might have said or done might give the clue. Spencer's quick hostility, MacLeod's open suspicion, Gaylord's vacillation—all those things might have been cloaks for their real intention. Mike Foley too, had been ardently urging the steel workers to go on strike, but had changed with abrupt suddenness when the Spider entered the picture.

Of course, the attitude of each of those men could easily be explained. Gaylord's vacillation pointed naturally to the fact that he knew his daughter to be in the hands of the ruthless criminal who controlled the mad men; Spencer's hostility might be due to his anxiety to keep the mills going; MacLeod's open suspicion had foundation in fact; and Mike Foley's quick change of heart could be attributed to the fact that he had supreme confidence in the Spider.

But *one* of those men must be acting a part. *One* of them was the head of this conspiracy.

Wentworth sighed. He had risked his life over and over again tonight, he had rescued Susan Gaylord from her captivity, he had beaten back the master of the madmen on every front tonight, but he was still no nearer a solution than when he had arrived in town.

Wearily, he climbed out through the window again, just as the tugboat bumped gently against the concrete abutment at the river bank. Charley Hendrix and Susan Gaylord were waiting for him.

"Let's get off," he said. "We'll go back to the city. I made their Number One man a promise that he would die within twenty-four hours. I mean to keep that promise!"

CHAPTER 7
A TRAP FOR NITA

BACK AT the unguarded barricade, past the dead bodies of the state police lying in gruesome silence along the river bank, a horde of men and women and children was pouring through the gate. They were fleeing from the city.

Word had spread everywhere that the south road was open, and the residents of Keystone seized the opportunity to escape

Wentworth sprang to the companion ladder, up which

desperadoes were swarming, guns in hand.

from the reign of terror which had engulfed them for the last week.

The thought that they might spread the epidemic to other parts of the country failed to halt them. They wanted only to get away from the danger of slaughter and pestilence. They plodded on foot, they rode crowded in autos and trucks, and some went on bicycles. The great exodus from the town of Keystone had begun.

The young woman whom Wentworth had failed to notice as he pursued the tugboat continued to drive her car toward the city, against this outflow of traffic. She was forced to hug the edge of the road, riding half in and half out of the ditch. Her progress was slow, and she eyed the fleeing throngs with wonder and apprehension. It was almost three quarters of an hour before she finally arrived at the corner of Main and Broad, opposite the City Hall. Setting out from her car, she crossed the street swiftly, and ascended the steps. She was tall, graceful and lithe, with a lively, vivacious beauty that caught the eyes of all who passed.

In the broad corridor of the City Hall building, she stopped for a moment, uncertain which way to go. A tall, middle-aged man who was just leaving the building noted her perplexity, and bowed, saying: "Can I help you?"

She flashed him a quick smile of gratitude. "If you can direct me to the office of Mayor Gaylord—"

The man bowed. "Glad to. You will have to wait, because he is in conference. Perhaps I can be of assistance to you. My name is Jonathan Spencer. I am the General Manager of the Keystone Steel & Iron Company."

"Oh, yes, Mr. Spencer. You—you are working with Mayor Gaylord to fight this dreadful calamity that has struck your city?"

He nodded. "I am doing everything I can. You are a stranger here?" Spencer's eyes were studying her carefully. "How did you get into the city?"

"The barricade was open. The state troopers were killed. I stopped a number of people to ask about it, but they all seemed in such a great hurry to leave town that I couldn't get a satisfactory answer. The people are trooping out of here in hordes."

"You have—business here?"

"Yes, Mr. Spencer. Since you are associated with Mayor Gaylord, I feel that I can tell you what I am here for. Naturally, it is to your interest to fight this thing. My name is Nita Van Sloan."

Spencer started perceptibly. "I've heard of you, Miss Van Sloan. You were associated with Commissioner Kirkpatrick in New York, at the time that he was fighting Tang-akhmut."

"That's true," she said eagerly. "I induced Commissioner Kirkpatrick to tell me—"

She stopped suddenly, as if she had said too much.

But Spencer smiled knowingly. "To tell you—what?"

"I mean," she faltered, "I mean, I got Commissioner Kirkpatrick's permission to come here. I want to help."

"You mean, don't you, that you induced Commissioner Kirkpatrick to tell you—where the Spider had gone?"

Nita's face assumed a poker expression. "*The Spider?*" she asked, as if she had never heard the name before. Spencer laughed lightly. "You needn't worry, Miss Van Sloan. I know

105

all about the Spider's coming here. In fact, Gaylord and I were anxious to have him help us. We shall be glad to have you with us, Miss Van Sloan. Come now, and I will introduce you to Gaylord."

NITA VAN SLOAN followed him down the corridor. She was thrilled with a sense of adventure, and of having done wrong. She knew very well that she should not have come. But where Wentworth went, she must also go.*

---

* AUTHOR'S NOTE: Readers of previous Spider stories have met Nita Van Sloan in the past. Beautiful and wealthy, she might have found herself a husband among the socially elect of the country and lived her life in the gilded boredom of a society matron. Instead she chose to follow Richard Wentworth along the road of peril and imminent death which he had chosen as a career. To live fully, swiftly, in the breath of daily adventure was the epitome of happiness for Nita Van Sloan when the fullness of life was achieved in company with the man she loved—Richard Wentworth. In the career of crime-fighting which he had chosen, he was estopped from offering Nita the quiet happiness of marriage and a home—and motherhood. But he gave her fully of the things which make life sweet to those who have been endowed with a high heart and shining courage: he gave her the privilege of participating in a game of danger, daring, excitement and thrill. Neither could have loved the other had they not both been constituted with a love of peril. Like gamblers staking their whole fortune on the carnival wheel, these two gloried in staking their lives. And if Wentworth would have preferred to see Nita Van Sloan safely at home while he risked life and limb, he had long ago given up hope of attempting to keep her out of the game. As was seen in a previous chapter, he had asked Kirkpatrick to keep from Nita the secret

Spencer entered the Mayor's office without knocking. Gaylord was sitting at his desk, conversing in low tones with Dr. MacLeod, who was bending over him. Gaylord frowned as he saw Spencer, then looked quizzically at Nita.

Spencer said: "I haven't abandoned the sentiments that I expressed to you a few minutes ago, Gaylord. The only reason I am returning is to escort this young lady here. I met her outside. She is—a friend of the person you sent for. You know whom I mean."

Gaylord grew taut. His eyes travelled over Nita, searching her face. "You mean—the Spider?" he asked of Spencer.

The General Manager of the Keystone plant nodded. "I didn't want to mention the Spider's name, because I didn't know whether you had let Dr. MacLeod into the secret. Apparently you have."

"Of course," Gaylord said petulantly. "Dr. MacLeod is the County Coroner. He is entitled to know what is going on." Nita stepped forward quickly. "Please, let's not argue and bicker." She stretched forth an appealing hand to Gaylord. "Now that you know what I've come here for, can you help me?"

Gaylord hesitated, glanced significantly at Jonathan Spencer.

Spencer bowed stiffly. "I understand." He turned to Nita. "You see, Miss Van Sloan, Gaylord and I don't see eye to eye in certain things. I insist that we must keep the shops open at all cost, while he feels that they should be closed."

of where he was going. But he might have known that she would wheedle it out of the Commissioner.

He waved his hand apologetically. "But I mustn't bother you with things like these. I'll leave now, so that Mayor Gaylord can tell you whatever he wants to, in confidence." He threw a scornful glance toward Gaylord and MacLeod, turned and stalked to the door. "Perhaps Dr. MacLeod is more to be trusted than I am."

When the door had closed behind Spencer, Nita took an impulsive step toward the desk. "I've been rash in coming here this way, Mayor Gaylord, but I couldn't rest until I knew whether the Spider was here. You must tell me—have you seen him?"

Gaylord shook his head. "I am sorry to say, Miss Van Sloan, that I haven't. But I know he's in town. He rescued Mr. Spencer, who just left, from an angry mob of steel workers. Since then he hasn't been heard from."

Dr. MacLeod came around the desk, put an arm on Nita's shoulder. "You shouldn't have come here, Miss Van Sloan. It's bad enough for those people who must remain in town. But for someone as beautiful as you to thrust yourself into the danger of epidemics and riots and slaughter—it's unthinkable. Come with me. I'll give you comfortable quarters in the hospital, and you can wait for news."

"Thank you," Nita said abstractedly. She was penitent, already regretting her hasty action in coming here, and thus disclosing her connection with the Spider. She would have given much to take back the things she had disclosed in the last ten minutes. But after all, her interest in the Spider did not necessarily implicate Richard Wentworth in any way. Though some might suspect his true identity, suspicion was not proof.

She allowed herself to be conducted from the room, and down the corridor where Dr. MacLeod showed her into a small waiting room. The door of the waiting room was open, and through it she could see the desk sergeant seated in the corridor.

Dr. MacLeod said: "If you will wait here a few moments, Miss Van Sloan, I'll finish up my business with Mayor Gaylord, and conduct you to the hospital."

He bent lower, and his voice dropped. "I may mention to you in passing, that I think I know where the Spider is. There was a gentleman here who gave the name of Dr. Benson. Somehow, I recollect Dr. Benson as looking differently from what this gentleman did. It may be that he is your friend, posing as Benson. In that case, I fully expect that he will visit the hospital. He will want to see the men who have been stricken with the epidemic of madness, whom we have under observation there. Your best chance of meeting him, therefore, will be to come with me."

NITA THANKED Dr. MacLeod, and he left her in the waiting room. Nervously, she lit a cigarette. Her mind was filled with a thousand conflicting ideas, and she was reproaching herself for doing the thing she had done. While she waited, she could see the desk sergeant busy over his phone, sending out hurry calls to patrolmen in other parts of the city, ordering them to rush to the South Road and set up the barricade once more before the city was emptied of its population.

Out on Main Street, people were excited, milling about, exchanging wild comments as to the nature of the events that had taken place within the last half hour. A steady stream of inhabitants was moving south on Main Street toward the south barricade.

Among the crowds, the small group of individuals whose clothing dripped water as if they had recently emerged from the river went unnoticed. These men drifted by twos and threes across the various bridges, over into the mill section. They all seemed to be converging upon an old, unused railroad shed alongside the siding. Soon there were almost a hundred of them closely packed in the old shed. These men were the ones who had escaped from the tugboat, *Miss Susan*.

They waited about in silence, a silence more ugly than any shouted threats might have been. Many of them held the small, compact Brownings which they had taken from the boat. They had carried these through the streets under their coats.

Now, as they waited a last figure vaulted up into the shed. The men stirred expectantly. It was their leader, the Russian, Gregory Bayer.

It could be seen that Bayer was in a towering rage. He pushed men aside indiscriminately, growling at them, and made his way across to the far corner of the shed. Here he bent and raised a trap-door, climbed down a short set of steps into a compartment underneath the floor of the shed.

"Two of you men come down here," he called up, "and get some of these bombs!"

Two of the men nearest the trap-door descended, and Bayer stepped over to a row of boxes snugly stuck into a corner. He pried the lid of the boxes open with a crowbar, revealing that the contents consisted of rows of grenades, packed closely together in straw. The men carried up four of the boxes under his direction, and then Bayer was left alone in the basement compartment. He stepped across to a radio set which had been installed in one corner, and set the dial, then spoke into the transmitter: "Number Two calling Number One. Number Two calling Number One."

He repeated the call several times, until suddenly that same rasping voice replied: "Number One on the air. Number Two, you have failed. You allowed the Spider to rout you from the tugboat. Now our plans are wrecked as far as Croton City is concerned. The epidemic has been planted there, and we were all ready for your men to come in and take charge. Where are you?"

"We are at sub-headquarters Number Four, sir," Bayer replied. "I am sorry that we failed, but I couldn't control the men. I was locked in the cabin. They swam ashore, and I figured they would come to this headquarters, because it's the only other one they know. Most of the men are here, and if there is anything we can do—"

"Yes. But you must act quickly. There is a young woman in the City Hall building now. Her name is Nita Van Sloan. She is five foot, five and a half, very beautiful, brown hair, a small nose. She is dressed in a gray tailored suit and a gray hat. You will take as many men as you need and proceed to the City Hall at once. Use whatever means you must, *but I want that girl captured!* Understand?"

"I understand, sir." It was one of Gregory Bayer's virtues, that he could grasp an order at once, and not ask unnecessary questions. "I'll start at once, sir. I expected action, and I distributed the gas grenades to the men."

"Very good. You will take her back to sub-headquarters Number Four, and then proceed with Alternate Plan Two. You know what that calls for?"

"Yes, sir. With the Brownings and the gas grenades, we should be able to carry out Alternate Plan Two. I'll report to you as soon as we reach our objective."

"All right, then. But do not fail this time, Bayer. I cannot excuse or overlook two failures in a row. Sign off." The rasping voice went off the air, Bayer removed the ear phones from his head.

He climbed up into the shed, and the men, who had begun to whisper among themselves, stopped and faced him expectantly.

"I want fifteen men." Bayer counted off the men that he wanted. "You will follow me. We'll have to commandeer a couple of cars on the way. The rest of you, wait here for my return. Be prepared for action."

Bayer and his fifteen men marched out into the night, while those who remained behind closed the sliding door of the shed. That shed had been gone through twice during the city-wide search for the hidden desperadoes and the kidnapped Susan Gaylord. But nobody had been inside, and none of the searchers had thought to look for a hidden trap door. All was silent along the river bank as Bayer and his men trickled across the Broad Street Bridge in the direction of the City Hall building, each with a couple of the gas grenades in his pocket, while half of them carried Browning submachine guns under their coats....

CHAPTER 8
THE ATTACK ON NO. 3

THE SPIDER, with Charley Hendrix and Susan Gaylord, had been compelled to halt at the barricade in the South Road. The crowd of fleeing residents was so thick that it was virtually impossible to get through. It was fifteen or twenty minutes before the city police arrived on the scene. They immediately closed the gate again, and set up a guard. But hundreds of people had already left the city, and hundreds of others gathered in a solid, compact mass, yelling and shouting to be permitted to leave.

Wentworth worked his coupé inside the barricade, and drove slowly through the milling throngs until he got out into Main Street.

Charley Hendrix sat with his arm around Susan, and the girl snuggled close to him. All three of them were wet and cold, and Hendrix had given Susan his coat, which was little comfort because it was still soaking wet from its immersion in the river.

Wentworth stared grimly ahead. He was trying to figure out logically what would be the next step of Number One in this campaign against the city. Thus far he had not been able to work out any tangible theory as to the motive behind the entire conspiracy. What could this Number One man possibly have to gain by spreading terror and madness through the town, and by slaughtering the steel workers *en masse?*

As the Spider, Wentworth had met many criminals of a high order of intelligence; and he had arrived at the conclusion that the basis of any criminal conspiracy lay generally in a very simple scheme. The cleverer the criminal, the more devious would be his way of attaining that simple goal. This was a perfect example of that thesis.

There was no question but that the Number One man at the head of this conspiracy was a very clever person. This so-called epidemic of madness and these unwarranted massacres of innocent steel workers and their families were, Wentworth was convinced, only smoke-screens to cover the true objective of Number One. The devilish part of it all—the clever part of it— was that Wentworth's activities must all be directed to combating these smoke-screen activities, whereas he would much have preferred to be free to delve deeper into the matter of the criminal's motive. One thing was certain—Number One was striking hard and fast, on the old theory that if you keep your enemy on the run he won't have time to organize.

Even now, as Wentworth drove up Main Street he was wondering where Number One would strike next. His answer came dramatically, startlingly. From the direction of the City Hall building there suddenly came to their ears the sharp, high-toned explosions of gas grenades, mingled with the quick, vicious rat-tat-tat of sub-machine guns. Once more the night was abruptly filled with sounds of battle.

Young Charley Hendrix pressed Susan Gaylord closer to him. "Good God!" he exclaimed, "they're attacking the City Hall! They've come across the river for the first time!"

Susan Gaylord moaned: "When will this murdering end?"

Wentworth said nothing. He stepped down on the accelerator, raced the coupé down Main Street, regardless of traffic obstructions.

The shooting continued, growing in crescendo. They were still some ten or twelve blocks from Broad Street, and as Wentworth kept his foot down on the accelerator he could imagine what was taking place there. Now he could glimpse the white City Hall building down the street, and could see crowded masses of panic-stricken people fleeing in every direction, could see clouds of smoke pouring from the City Hall building, while above everything could be heard the continuous staccato barks of the sub-machine guns.

ABRUPTLY, A compact group of men dashed out of the City Hall building. It was too far yet to see their faces, but Wentworth could guess who they were. He could see a man in the lead carrying an inert form over his shoulder. It was the figure of a woman. Wentworth's lips tightened. Whom were they abducting this time? He could not guess that it was Nita Van Sloan. He had not seen her come to the city and he was relying on the fact that Kirkpatrick had promised not to divulge his whereabouts.

Hendrix gasped: "Hurry, Spider. Hurry!"

"This is as fast as we can go," Wentworth told him. "I'm afraid we can't make it."

He was right. The compact group of men had spread, and were entering three automobiles at the curb. Sprays of machine-gun bullets swept the crowd in the streets, mowing them down, clearing the way for the three cars as they sped into the night directly across the Broad Street Bridge.

The whole thing was over almost as soon as it had begun.

Wentworth raced down Main Street, swung to the left over the Broad Street Bridge, a good four blocks behind the fleeing sedan.

Charley Hendrix, looking behind, said with bated breath: "They've killed dozens of people! And they must have used gas grenades in the building. Look at that smoke coming out of it!"

Wentworth sent his coupé speeding after the sedan, twisting in and out of dark, deserted streets in the mill district. The rear car of the three suddenly braked to a stop, and the snout of a sub-machine gun was poked out through the rear window, smashing the glass. At once, slugs began to rip down the street at Wentworth's coupé. They beat against the shatter-proof windshield, cracking it into a thousand criss-cross lines; they smashed into the radiator, ripped the tires, and both of the front shoes went with a great explosion. The coupé veered, swerved. Wentworth fought the wheel madly but before he could bring the car to a stop it had skidded in a complete turn. The fleeing gun men did not wait to finish their job. Apparently they were satisfied to stop pursuit. The sedan lurched forward after the first two, disappeared into the night even while Wentworth was leaping out of his coupé.

No one came out to see what was the matter. Farther east, the blast furnaces and the open hearths sent up their streaks of fire into the night, accompanied by the incessant clanging of the huge hydraulic presses. The mills were working, and the slight flurry of machine-gun fire was drowned by the noise of steel manufacture.

Grimly, Richard Wentworth stared into the night after the

fleeing sedan. "Come on," he called to Hendrix and Susan Gaylord. "We're going to the union headquarters. I think this thing is heading for a show-down!"

He started off, walking at a brisk pace, leaving the other two to follow him. His mind was working swiftly, coping with every angle of the problem.

An attack upon the City Hall building was the last thing which he had expected the Number One man to order. Such an attack would force the hand of Gaylord, would arouse public sentiment throughout the state to such a pitch that the Governor would step in whether he was requested to do so or not. It seemed to him that things must be drawing to a head, or else that the Number One man had been driven to a desperate measure by the loss of the tugboat.

Whatever the situation, Wentworth was convinced that a crisis was approaching. In such a crisis he wanted the cooperation of the steel workers whom he had armed. He left Hendrix and Susan Gaylord far behind as his long, swinging drive carried him through the night.

IN THE meantime, the three fleeing cars containing the gun men had swung off to the south, and cut back in a wide circle toward the railroad shed.

Gregory Bayer climbed down from the first car, carrying the inert figure of Nita Van Sloan across his shoulder. A red gash at the side of her temple indicated how she had been treated.

At a signal from Bayer, the sliding door of the shed was pushed open, and the desperadoes crowded within, climbed out.

Bayer handed Nita's body to two of his men, and they placed

her in the back of one of the cars. Then the Russian issued swift orders. The gunmen crowded into the three cars, hanging on running boards and clinging to spare tires on the back. Those who could not be accommodated formed into a group and set off on foot behind the three slowly moving cars. They cut across the mill district toward the north end, where open hearth shop Number Three was situated.

They stopped in the shadow, about a hundred yards from the entrance to the shop, shrouded by the night from the view of the small guard of policemen at the entrance. Bayer issued further orders, and twenty of the men, each armed with a sub-machine gun, crept forward. The others followed at a short distance, one of the men carrying Nita. When the advance guard was within fifty feet of the gate, one of the police spotted them, and called out a nervous challenge: "Who goes there?"

Bayer rapped out a quick order, and the guard challenged was answered by a hail of machine-gun slugs that swept the police guards off their feet, cutting them down mercilessly. The night reverberated with the vicious spitting of machine guns. Bayer issued another order, and the entire contingent of desperadoes rushed forward. One of the men hurled a bomb at the gate, and it exploded with a shocking detonation, shattering the obstruction, and clearing the path for the charge.

The desperadoes raced through that gate, and were met by three more policemen within the grounds. The three were also armed with sub-machine guns, but they could not stand against the superior force. They were mowed down before they could fire a shot.

Bayer's ruthless gunmen swept over their dead bodies, and stormed the entrance of open hearth shop Number Three. The steel workers were taken by surprise. The desperadoes swept into line just within the entrance, their Brownings covering everybody in the huge room. The Russian's eyes were glittering avidly.

"Kill! Kill!" he shouted.

The gun men pressed the trips of their machine guns, and the echoes of the chattering bursts rebounded from the high ceilings of the shops, as steel workers fell before that hail of slugs. Here and there an isolated worker ran in panic-stricken dread, seeking safety; but they were all cut down by the Brownings before they could get out of the big room. The shop was in the hands of the gun men.

Gregory Bayer's thin lips twisted into a wicked smile. He raced across the shop to a door marked "Office." He ripped open the door, and his revolver spoke three times in quick succession. Three slugs crashed into the body of the white-faced shop manager who had arisen from behind a desk. The manager was hurled backward into his chair, and sat there, head thrown back, blood spurting from the three great wounds.

Bayer did not vouchsafe a second glance for the men he had killed. He reached across the dead body, snapped up the telephone, and spoke a number into the transmitter. He waited a moment, then when he got his connection, he spoke triumphantly.

"I guess it's all right to call you on the telephone now, Number One. This is Number Two reporting. Alternate Plan Number

Two is a complete success. We have the girl, and we have complete control of open hearth shop Number Three."

Over the phone came that familiar rasping voice of Number One: "Good, Bayer. You will hold the shop as long as you can. There is enough food and ammunition in the store room to hold you for a week. But you need remain only another day or so. Our operation should be completed within twenty-four hours. Do not use the telephone again. You will find complete radio equipment hooked up in the storeroom. Use that."

"Very good, sir," Bayer replied. "Do you want me to proceed with the other element of Alternate Plan Number Two?"

"Yes, yes, by all means. You will send out small raiding parties to bomb the other plants. You must cause as much havoc and destruction within the next two days as you possibly can."

Bayer asked: "What about our getaway when we're through? You're sure the underground passage is open?"

"It's open all the way through to the South End Bus Terminal. There will be two big buses at the terminal, capable of taking you all out of town. Now hang up. Report to me by radio hereafter."

Bayer replaced the instrument on the hook, went out into the shop. His men had spread around in the huge room, and were callously carrying the bodies of the dead steel workers and dumping them in a corner. The open hearth furnaces were glowing redly, with the molten steel ready to pour, but there were no workers to tend them. Their temperature was rising swiftly, threatening to burn through the stoppers in the vents. But none of the desperadoes paid any attention to that. They had laid Nita Van Sloan upon the floor, and she was stirring, with returning consciousness. Bayer strode across the room, picking out three groups of ten men each.

"Go down to the storeroom in the basement," he ordered, "and supply yourselves with bombs. You will find them stored there in boxes marked 'Machinery.' You will form into three raiding parties and spread out through the mill district. Each group will take one of the cars outside, and make a swift raid. Do as much damage as you can, then return here at once."

While they were obeying his instructions and getting ready to leave on the raid, Bayer stepped across to Nita Van Sloan, watched her dazedly trying to focus her gaze upon the strange scene. His forefinger stroked the ugly scar on his cheek.

"So you are the Spider's woman, eh?" he said softly. "Maybe the Spider won't like what we're going to do to you, lady; but it'll be fun. Ha, ha. Plenty of fun!"

CHAPTER 9
NO QUARTER ASKED!

RICHARD WENTWORTH reached Union head-quarters far ahead of Hendrix and Susan Gaylord. In fact, he had walked so fast that the two young lovers were blocks behind him. Wentworth had removed from the wrecked coupé the hat and cloak of the Spider, and he donned these before turning the corner. There were four steel workers on guard at the headquarters' entrance, and upon seeing him they all stood to attention, like trained soldiers.

Wentworth smiled. Mike Foley must have been working

on them in the short time since they had acquired weapons, trying to whip them into shape to meet organized crime with organized vigilance. And Foley had done a good job. Upstairs in the big meeting room where Jonathan Spencer had almost been mobbed a short while ago, the main body of the steel workers were sitting about, conversing in groups. Mike Foley had rigged up a desk on the platform, and he was transacting his business from there.

It was strange to see the twisted, caped and hatted figure of the Spider walk through a room full of men, unmolested. Even Wentworth felt the novelty of the situation. Hitherto, he had always been hunted by the law, as well as by the underworld. It was a novelty to him to enjoy, in the identity of the Spider, the respect and admiration of law-abiding men.

122

A low cheer went up from the steel workers as Wentworth passed down the aisle, and mounted the platform. Mike Foley leaped up, smiling broadly. "We were worried about you, Spider. We almost decided to go out and see did you need any help."

Wentworth waved a hand. He spoke brusquely. "I think things are coming to a head, Foley. The Number One Man has been driven into the open at last. Apparently he must strike swiftly now, or all his plans will crumble. I want you to send out scouts, to cover every section of the mill district. Keep the main body of men in readiness to go wherever trouble breaks—" He was interrupted by the distant sounds of machine-gun fire, carrying fitfully through the night above the noises of the shops.

Foley exclaimed: "That sounds like they've started already! It's from the east—right from Open Hearth Shop Number Three, where the trouble originally started!"

The *rat-tat-tat* of continuous machine gunning continued, rising in intensity. Abruptly it ceased, and after an instant there was a terrific detonation, as of a bomb.

Wentworth said crisply: "All right, men, we needn't wait any longer. Let's go!"

He leaped down from the platform, raced to the door, and down the staircase, with the steel workers trooping after him. In the street, they once more heard the quick sharp bursts of Brownings.

"It's Number Three Shop, all right!" Foley shouted.

Wentworth broke into a swift lope in the direction of the shooting, followed by the now eager steel men. They were anxious to come to blows with the desperadoes who had terrorized the town, and who had killed friends and relatives of theirs. Brownings or no Brownings, these men were ready to fight.

Open Hearth Shop Number Three was only a few blocks north of where they were. The main company plant was located at Broad Street, almost directly across the river from the Keystone City Hall. The open hearth shops and the blast furnaces were spread out over the North End, and as Wentworth and his men ran through the night, their numbers were augmented by workers from other shops, who had heard the firing.

NOW, AS they approached Number Three, they were suddenly met by a blaze of machine-gun fire from the grounds outside the shop. Luckily, the gunmen under Gregory Bayer had opened up just a little bit too soon, and the steel workers were still out of range.

Wentworth shouted: "Spread out! Keep your distance. Get down!"

The men dropped to the ground, taking cover wherever it was afforded, while steel-jacketed slugs from the Brownings whistled harmlessly in the street. Wentworth knew that his men, with their automatics, were no match for the gunmen armed with their high-powered Brownings. If they were to charge, they would be cut down mercilessly.

Foley wriggled over to him, where he lay hugging a hydrant. "What'll we do, Spider?" Foley shouted. "Do we go in and smash 'em?"

"No. You'd be cut down before you could reach the gate!"

From where he lay, he could see the breach in the fence, where the gate had been blown away by the bomb. "Those men have bombs as well as machine guns. We'll have to try taking them in the rear. You stay here with half the men. I'll take the other half and work around to the back."

With the machine gun slugs still ripping down the street, Wentworth crawled about among the men, picking his contingent. "When you hear firing from the rear," he told Foley, "you begin your advance on this side. Crawl forward, firing as you go. But don't get reckless. If the machine gun barrage gets too strong for you, stop."

"Like hell we'll stop!" Foley growled. "The boys are good and sore now. They're bent on cleaning these guys out for good!"

"Let's hope we can do it," Wentworth said. He raised his arm in signal, and began to run, crouching, around the side of the fence. The men he had selected followed him.

Around on the west side, there was another narrow gate in the fence, through which ran the single gauge track upon which iron ore was hauled up from the river. This track ran east and west, serving seven or eight open hearth shops along its route.

Just as Wentworth rounded the corner, he saw a small group of the gunmen running toward the narrow gate, dragging two prisoners. He recognized those two at once—Charley Hendrix and Susan Gaylord. They had been picked up by one of the raiding parties that had gone out at Bayer's order. They had fallen so far behind Wentworth that they had lost him, and had wandered around in the mill district till they were caught.

Now, Wentworth called to his men: "Don't shoot. That's Mayor Gaylord's daughter and her fiancé that they've got there!"

He crawled forward, watching while the gate over the narrow

gauge track was opened to permit the entry of the raiding party. They could see that a strong guard was posted here as well as at the front, armed with the Brownings. It would be folly to attack in the face of those machine guns.

Swiftly Wentworth went over the situation in his mind, while the steel workers crowded around him in the night. From the front of the shop they could still hear sporadic firing. The gunmen had realized that Foley's men were still out of range, and they were merely sending an occasional burst in their direction to make them keep their distance.

Wentworth frowned, puzzled. He couldn't understand why the Number One Man, whoever he was, should have ordered his desperadoes to seize and hold one of the mills. A thing like this would surely bring down martial law upon the town, whether Gaylord asked for it or not; and since the Number One Man knew that Susan Gaylord was out of his hands, he must know that Gaylord would hesitate no longer about calling on the governor for assistance. He could not have known that Susan would be recaptured. Wentworth could only assume that the next few hours meant everything to the plans of Number One. Therefore, the shop must be captured, and the desperadoes driven out. But how? They were too well armed.

One of the men crowding around him asked: "What do we do now, Spider? Say the word and we'll rush the gate—"

Wentworth laughed harshly. "And be slaughtered like cattle! No, we've got to find some way—"

Suddenly he snapped his fingers. "By God, I've got it!" His eyes, travelling through the darkness, had spotted the bulk of an electric locomotive hooked up to half a dozen freight cars, standing idly on a siding some two hundred yards away.

"Follow me!" he shouted.

AS THEY began to run toward the locomotive, the gunmen inside the gate spotted them and opened fire with the Brownings. Slugs whined through the air, bit into the ground at their feet, and four or five of the steel workers fell, mortally shot, before they got out of range. The gunmen inside the gate yelled derisively after them.

Now Wentworth was close to the train. He climbed up into the locomotive, with the steel workers swarming up after him.

"Spread out through the train," he ordered, "and be ready for the shock when we crash the gate!"

The men grasped the idea with enthusiasm. Half a dozen of them volunteered to drive the engine, and Wentworth assigned two for that honor. He posted himself in the cab, made sure that all of his men were aboard, then gave the word. The engine started, dragging the freight cars behind it.

"There's only about two hundred yards to go," Wentworth told Harry Sellers, the man at the throttle. "Get up as much speed as you can."

Sellers nodded, sent the engine rolling forward. "I don't know if I can get up enough momentum to crash the gate, Spider, but I'll try."

The train rumbled down the narrow gauge track with dreadful slowness. Wentworth groaned. They would never get up enough steam in that short distance. The gunmen inside the gate had become aware of what was taking place, and they were firing systematically at the engine. Bullets whisked around the cab, *sponging* against the metal of the locomotive.

Wentworth reached over and pressed the button which controlled the headlight. The powerful beam cut through the night, illuminated the interior of the grounds behind the fence, showed them the gunmen kneeling and firing their Brownings, and other gunmen running out from the building to support them. The narrow gauge track ran up close alongside the shop, where a loading platform jutted out to receive the shipments of ore.

Now the engine was almost upon the gate. Suddenly, under Harry Sellers' manipulation, it spurted forward, smashed ponderously into the iron framework. That last spurt was what did the trick. The gate crumbled under the impact, and the train rolled into the yard!

The gunmen were on either side of it, firing up at the cab and at the freight cars. Wentworth and his steel workers returned the fire with their automatics. Battle raged in the night, and the flashes of the guns followed each other so swiftly that one might have thought them a continuous blast of flame. The headlight was shot out by a spray of machine gun bullets, just as the train rolled to a stop against the loading platform.

The steel workers, from the protection of the freight cars, swept the yard with a continuous barrage from their automatics, sending the gunmen to cover.

Wentworth leaped from the cab, landed on all fours on the platform. A man with a Browning gun, just inside the shop, saw him and raised the tommy to his shoulder. Wentworth shot the man through the forehead, sprang forward into the shop. He raced through the receiving rooms, which were deserted, then entered a corridor where two of the gunmen were running toward the loading platform. Both men had machine guns, but before they could use them in the cramped quarters, Wentworth's automatics spoke twice, and the two men fell away before him as if blown down in a gale.

Wentworth kicked the Brownings out of the way, ran on. Another man might have stopped to pick up one of those submachine guns. Not the Spider. He knew that if there were going to be shooting in the big shop, it would have to be close shooting, for he knew that the gunmen had prisoners. A machine gun is all right when you are facing a massed enemy; but it's no good when you have to shoot carefully, when you have to avoid hitting friends among the enemy.

He didn't bother to see whether his men were behind him, whether he was cut off from them. Now the Spider was in his proper element, fighting the kind of fight that he gloried in— one man with blazing automatics against many.

He burst into the great shop honeycombed with the tracks of its overhead travelling cranes, with the heat of the open hearths spreading its hot breath to every corner. Swiftly he gazed about, summed up the situation. He saw the pile of bodies in a corner— the dead bodies of the workers who had been massacred when the gunmen seized the shop. He saw the desperadoes massed at the door, fighting back a group of steel workers who had stormed the front entrance while Wentworth created his diversion at the rear.

The Spider smiled grimly. Now he could have no more doubts as to Foley's integrity, for he saw the big union president locked in hand-to-hand struggle in the doorway with one of the gunmen.

And then his smile faded. There, across the vast room, he saw something that sent a chill of horror up his spine in spite of the heat of the place. Nita Van Sloan was lying on her face on the floor, directly in front of one of the open hearth furnaces!

Near by, the big Russian, Gregory Bayer, was supervising four of his men who were trundling a flat conveyor toward the open door of another of the furnaces. Upon that conveyor were tied two figures—Charley Hendrix and Susan Gaylord!

THE CONVEYOR was intended for trundling ore into the furnaces. When the conveyor entered the furnace, its slab-like top could be raised to an angle which would cause the ore to slide into the furnace. But instead of ore, the conveyor now carried the figures of Susan Gaylord and Charley Hendrix.

The four gunmen under Bayer's direction were pushing the conveyor toward the furnace. Charley and Susan were tied hand and foot, on their backs in such manner that they could not move. The open door of the furnace irradiated a heat so intense that the faces of the two captives as well as the four gunmen appeared supernaturally ruddy to Wentworth from where he stood, across the vast room. Nita Van Sloan, too, as she lay on the floor, gave the impression of a sun bather lying on the broiling beach in Miami—except that the peacefulness of the southern beach was lacking from this scene of terror and confusion.

Bayer, his ugly scar showing red in the glow from the furnaces, was ordering the men to shove the conveyor into the oven. In a moment the bodies of Susan and Charley would be shriveled, consumed, reduced to ashes. They were straining against their bonds, twisting their heads in frantic terror.

And Wentworth raised his two automatics, fired carefully and accurately four times in swift succession. His shots mingled with the explosions of other automatics outside, and with the shouts and curses of the embattled men in the doorway. The four desperadoes at the conveyor fell away from it ludicrously, one after the other, as the four slugs found their marks unerringly. Abruptly, the conveyor ceased moving. Molten steel squirmed like live lava within the furnace, seeming to writhe in impotent wrath at having been cheated of its prey.

Susan and Charley could not seem to understand what had given them a respite from the dreadful death toward which they had been moving. They twisted their heads to get a better view, and their eyes opened wide as they saw the Spider at the far end of the room.

Other desperadoes came running toward the conveyor at the shouted command of Gregory Bayer. They stooped to push the conveyor. The Russian had raised his gun to fire at the Spider, but appalled at Wentworth's uncannily accurate aim, he leaped to one side, seized Nita Van Sloan by the hair, and dragged her up from the floor, holding her as a shield in front of himself. Nita was only half conscious, and the fiery flames from the open hearth threw a weird, ruddy glow over the soft white skin of her body, which was exposed where the Russian had ripped her dress away.

Bayer held her up, his thick fingers twisted in her glorious hair. She was just conscious enough to feel the pain of that tugging against her hair. She swayed on her feet, with her dress ripped open at the breasts. Bayer raised his gun again, fired at Wentworth from behind her body.

Now Wentworth glanced behind him, saw that his own men were storming through the corridor toward the shop. Apparently the fury of their rage had prevailed against the Brownings, at close quarters. They had broken through the gunmen at the loading platform. At the front door, the desperadoes and the steel men were still locked in deadly conflict, neither side yielding an inch. They were too close for shooting now, and they were slugging with clubbed revolvers, gouging and kicking. No quarter was being asked or given in this grim battle.

A slug from Bayer's gun ricocheted from the floor, almost at Wentworth's feet. Wentworth raised his gun to answer, but held his fire. At that distance, not even he could hope to hit Bayer without endangering Nita's life. Wentworth glanced desperately about, saw a crane directly above his head, suspended from tracks that ran directly to the open hearth before which Bayer stood, and into which Susan and Charley were once more being trundled.

Bayer's shots were coming closer now, and several of the gunmen had detached themselves from the fight at the doorway, had spotted the caped and cloaked figure, and were shouting: "It's the Spider! Get the Spider!"

THEY OPENED up with their revolvers, and one of them raised a Browning, placed a finger on the trip.

Wentworth leaped backward, to where a switch in the wall controlled the power of the travelling crane. Ordinarily these cranes were controlled from a main cubbyhole, but each crane had its own emergency switch, which could operate it in case of necessity. If only the power had been left on in the line!... Wentworth threw the switch.

Bullets thudded into the wall beside him as the Browning opened upon him. He paid them no attention, but eagerly watched the crane.

It began to move. The power was on!

Wentworth bent his knees, went into a flying leap, and grasped the hook of the crane, drew his knees up and rode with it across the room!

The man with the Browning swung the muzzle of his machine gun to cut Wentworth down. But the crane was moving swiftly enough to delay his aiming. Wentworth snapped a shot with his free hand, and the machine gunner toppled backward with a gaping hole in his chest. Now Wentworth concentrated his fire upon the four men trundling the conveyor, regardless of the slugs that whined past him from Bayer's gun. He brought down two of them, firing with almost miraculous accuracy from the now swiftly moving crane. The other two let go of the conveyor and turned to run, at sight of the fate which had overtaken their fellows.

Ordinarily, one man attacking them would not have meant anything to these hardened gunmen. But they had all heard of the Spider; and that caped figure, riding the overhead crane and shooting with deadly marksmanship, reminded them of the grisly stories they had heard in the dark corners of the under-world—how no man could hope to escape the vengeance of the Spider; how the Spider's blazing guns had brought death to the boldest and the most dangerous of criminals. And the Spider's reputation, as much as his uncanny shooting, won the day. Those two turned and fled toward the doorway rather than trade shots with the man the underworld dreaded.

But not Gregory Bayer.

Safe behind the protection of Nita's body, he raised his gun once more, aimed carefully, coldly. His finger compressed on the trigger, and Wentworth could see that the Russian had a dead bead on him, was following him with a steady hand. Bayer's shot could not miss, and Wentworth dared not try to fire at him, shielded behind Nita. The Spider, hanging by one arm from that travelling crane, stared death in the eye, and could do nothing about it.

But just as Bayer was about to pull the trigger, Nita intervened. The pain of Bayer's grip on her hair had brought her back to full consciousness, and she saw what was happening. She twisted about, clenching her hands against the excruciating pain at the roots of her hair, and sank her teeth into Bayer's wrist.

The Russian screamed with the sudden pain. The gun was deflected, exploding into the floor. Nita kept her teeth in his wrist, and he dropped the gun, let go his grip on her hair, and slugged her on the top of the head with his knotted fist. Nita gasped, and her jaws opened, fell away from Bayer's wrist. The Russian hit her again, stepped back as she sagged to the floor.

He glanced up in sudden terror at the black figure of the Spider, which had come directly over his head on the travelling crane.

Wentworth's gun was empty. He flung it away, leaped down at the Russian. Bayer's hand slid inside his coat to the sheath strapped at his chest, and came out with the flashing, keen-edged knife that he always carried.

Wentworth landed on his feet, and he launched himself at the Russian. Bayer lunged upward with his knife, in the blow he constantly practiced. With that lunge he had often disemboweled an antagonist. But this antagonist was different from the others. Wentworth was experienced in the deadly methods of waterfront fighting as well as in more conventional methods. He had seen men disemboweled by that stroke, in street fighting in Singapore, and in riots in Canton and Shanghai.

Instead of retreating before the deadly blade, he stepped forward and to one side. The knife swished past him, stabbing up into empty air; and he caught Bayer's knife hand in a power-ful grip, twisted abruptly, mercilessly. The Russian howled with sudden agony as his wrist snapped like a dry shell. The knife dropped from nerveless fingers, and Wentworth rocked him back with a hard blow to the jaw. Bayer tottered, taking two involuntary steps backward. He brought up against the white hot surface of the open hearth, and screamed, began to dance on the floor.

Now Wentworth's face paled under the make-up of the Spider. He saw that a stray bullet had struck the vent of the furnace, and the molten steel was pouring out, on the floor. Usually a huge cylindrical bucket was placed at the mouth of the vent to receive the hot flow of wriggling metal. Now the bucket was not there, and the liquid steel was spreading in a small, seething, white-hot lake over the floor. It was this that Bayer had stepped into. The steel had bitten right through his shoes, and he screamed with agony, leaped away, but tripped and dropped full in the river of steel.

He squirmed, twisted, screaming, flailing with his broken wrist. His agony lasted but a moment, for no living organism can survive the shock of a first degree burn administered by molten steel. In an instant he stopped flailing the air, and lay still in the fiery bath of metal, his flesh sizzling terribly. He was dead! WENTWORTH GLANCED at the conveyor, saw that Susan and Charley were far enough from the furnace to be safe, then swung toward where Nita lay.

He uttered a cry of dismay. She was dazedly struggling to her knees. The edge of the lake of molten steel was slowly oozing toward her, barely a foot away. In a moment it would be lapping at her limbs. Wentworth leaped toward her, lifted her bodily, and carried her away from the sizzling river of fire.

"Nita, darling!" he exclaimed.

Her eyes opened and she smiled. "Dick! I'm always getting into trouble—and you're always there to get me out!"

He kissed her, set her on her feet, looked around for the automatic he had dropped from the crane. It was right in the middle of the flowing steel, beside the body of Gregory Bayer.

He shrugged, took out his second automatic and inserted a clip with swift, steady fingers. But that was unnecessary. The gunmen at the door, seeing the death of their leader, had lost heart, and were throwing down their arms in surrender. The steel workers under Foley took them prisoner, none too gently. From the rear, the men who had followed Wentworth came trooping in, also with prisoners. The victory was complete!

Wentworth walked carefully around the river of steel, reached out for the conveyor upon which Susan and Charley were tied, and dragged it out into the center of the room. Foley produced a knife and cut them loose.

The steel workers were celebrating wildly, jubilantly, crowding around Wentworth, patting his back and shaking his hand. Nita, partially recovered from her ordeal, had her arms around Susan, and was comforting her, while Charley Hendrix looked on with a dazed expression, hardly believing that he and Susan had really escaped the fiery death in the furnace.

Foley said to Wentworth: "What now, Spider? We've cleaned up here. What do we do next?"

Wentworth said soberly: "We've cleaned up, all right. But we still don't know who the Number One Man is. That man must be eliminated!"

"But—how you going to do that?"

"I'll show you. Get your men out of here. I want to be alone with Bayer's body for a few minutes."

Foley didn't understand, but he complied, ordering the men out, sending a small party to stand guard at each gate. Wentworth had told him to do that, saying: "I'd like to keep the news of this victory a secret for another hour—long enough for me to try a little plan."

He was left alone with Nita and the body of Bayer. Even Charley Hendrix and Susan Gaylord went out.

Nita watched him while he took out his make-up case, and carefully set to work. Bayer was lying face up, and though his body was sizzling revoltingly, his face with his ugly scar, remained untouched. Wentworth used pigment, nose plates and facial creams, turning every few minutes to study the dead Russian's features. At the end of five minutes he sighed, and stood up. "What do you think of it?" he asked Nita.

"Marvelous!" she gasped. "If I hadn't seen you do it, I'd think I was looking at the Russian!"

He chuckled. "It's because you're so wrought up, Nita. No man can disguise himself to pass accurately for another. But this scar—" he touched the long streak he had simulated upon his left cheek—"helps with the delusion. It'll be good enough to serve for what I have in mind tonight—I hope!"

He raised his voice, called to Foley: "All right, Foley. I'm ready. Get me a car, and four men to drive into town. We're going to pay a call—on Number One!"

HALF AN hour later, Wentworth, minus his cape and hat, emerged from a sedan at the back entrance of the City Hall. Inside the car were the four men he had brought with him, as well as Susan Gaylord and Charley Hendrix.

"Come with me, Charley," he said. "I think I'll be needing you."

On the way into the City Hall Building, Wentworth asked Charley: "You're connected with Hendrix, MacIntyre & Hendrix, aren't you?"

Charley nodded. "My father and my uncle own the firm. We've had seats on the stock exchanges of every large center, for almost thirty years."

"Do you carry stock trading accounts for any of the executives of the Keystone Steel & Iron Corporation?"

"Of course. We have Spencer's account, Gaylord's, and almost every other director and executive."

"How is the stock of the Keystone Corporation these days?"

"Well, its fallen off about fifty percent since this business started. But all the stock that's being dumped on the market is being absorbed by the directors. Gaylord and Spencer are using every nickel of their personal fortunes to buy all the stock that's offered, in order to keep the bottom from dropping out of it."

"I see," Wentworth said softly.

They walked through the wide corridor leading to the executive offices.

Charley Hendrix threw a side glance at Wentworth. "God!" he said in a hushed voice. "If I didn't know you were the Spider, I'd almost swear I was walking alongside of that Russian. That scar looks just like his. I can't believe its only paint."

Wentworth squeezed Charley's arm. "Quiet. Here comes Spencer. Duck around the corner. I want to talk to him alone."

Charley Hendrix saw Jonathan Spencer coming down the corridor, and he quickly stepped away from Wentworth, stepped around the corner. Spencer was apparently walking toward Mayor Gaylord's office, and there seemed to be something weighty on his mind, for he was gazing abstractedly at the floor. He did not see Wentworth until the Spider said: "Good evening, Mr. Spencer."

Spencer looked up startled, then his brow furrowed. He stepped back in alarm. "You—you're the man that led those murderers on the raid tonight! Help—"

He raised his voice to shout, but Wentworth stepped in quickly, placed a hand over his mouth. "Silence! You won't be hurt!" He placed a gun against Spencer's ribs. "Move back around the corner!"

Spencer hesitated, and Wentworth poked him again with the gun. "No harm will come to you if you obey."

Spencer stuttered: "W-what are you going to do? Haven't you done enough damage? God—"

"That's enough!" Wentworth hustled him around the corner, to where Hendrix was standing. "Take care of Mr. Spencer, Charley," he ordered. "Keep him out of circulation for ten minutes. And you can explain to him while you're waiting, that I'm not the villain he thinks I am!"

Charley nodded, drew his own gun and covered Spencer.

Wentworth left them, walked down the corridor to the mayor's office, turned the knob and entered without rapping.

Gaylord and Doctor MacLeod were sitting at the desk, and Gaylord was talking into the telephone: "Your son is all right, Mr. Hendrix. Now about that stock. I want you to buy everything that's offered. It'll drop some more tomorrow, I'm afraid—"

He stopped, his eyes staring as if at a ghost, fixed upon the apparition of Wentworth in the doorway. MacLeod followed his glance, uttered a startled oath, and sprang up.

Gaylord said into the phone: "Excuse me, Hendrix. Something important has come up. I'll call you later." He hung up, got to his feet, and asked coldly: "What brings you here?"

WENTWORTH GRINNED, and simulated the voice of Bayer. He was glad that there was only a single light on the desk, for it helped his disguise. "I had to come," he said. "I tried to get you on the radio, but there was no answer. We were attacked at Number Three Shop, and all my men are killed or captured. The game's up."

Gaylord glanced at MacLeod, then looked at Wentworth. "How—how did you know to come here? How did you know—"

"That you are the Number One Man?"

Gaylord nodded weakly.

Wentworth laughed harshly. "You don't think Gregory Bayer is a fool, do you? I like to know whom I work for. And it's a damn good thing I did, because otherwise I wouldn't have been able to get in touch with you now. I tried that telephone number that I used earlier in the night, but it didn't answer."

"That's right," said Gaylord. "That was Doctor MacLeod's phone. He has it tapped into a public telephone, so it can't be traced. He hasn't been there tonight, because we expected to hear from you on the radio. But quick—why did you fail?"

"That damn Spider. I have to admit he's too clever for me. I'm afraid the game's up, Gaylord!"

"No, no!" Gaylord shouted. "We're in too deep now. MacLeod and I are buying every bit of Keystone stock on margin. By tomorrow we'll control the whole corporation—with stock bought at bargain prices. We've got to keep up this terrorization for another twenty-four hours at all costs!"

MacLeod broke in: "But how can we, Gaylord? Isn't it risking too much—"

Gaylord turned on MacLeod furiously: "Risking too much! You fool! Haven't we risked everything already? Didn't I risk my own daughter in the hands of Bayer, so that Spencer would think I was being forced into standing by supinely? Didn't you risk your reputation when you injected that coma-producing drug into the men you vaccinated, and then hypnotized them so they'd go berserk at a certain time? What more have we to lose?"

Just then the door was pushed violently open, and Jonathan Spencer strode in, followed by Charley Hendrix, who looked crestfallen. Young Hendrix spread his hands apologetically to Wentworth. "I couldn't hold him, after I'd explained who you were," he said. "Spencer dared me to shoot, and of course I couldn't kill him in cold blood."

Spencer smiled warmly at Wentworth. "By God, Spider, you're clever! I want to thank you for everything you've done for the town!" He turned to Gaylord and MacLeod. "Look here, Gaylord, this man is perfectly all right. Charley Hendrix told me all about it. He's the Spider, and he's disguised himself as that damned Russian in order to trap the criminal behind all this. I'm sure we'll all help him—"

Wentworth sighed. "You're an honest man, Spencer, but you certainly know how to put your foot in it. *These two are the criminals!*"

Gaylord and MacLeod had been listening almost with stupe-faction to Spencer's innocent disclosure. Gaylord was the first to recover. Suddenly he was a snarling beast at bay as he reached into the open drawer of his desk and brought out a long-bar-reled forty-five.

"The Spider!" he snarled. *"Kill them, MacLeod, and our secret remains safe!"*

MacLeod was not slow to grasp the situation, and his own hand flashed in and out of his shoulder holster, came out with a snub-nosed automatic. But before either of them could fire, Wentworth's two automatics had appeared in his hands mirac-ulously. They spat spitefully twice, and a round, black hole appeared in the forehead of each of the two super-criminals.

Richard Wentworth stood stiffly while MacLeod and Gaylord sank to the floor, dead.

Then, while Spencer and Hendrix watched open-mouthed, he stepped forward, manipulated with a platinum cigarette lighter, while bending over the two still-warm bodies. When he arose, Spencer and Hendrix could see that the forehead of each, alongside the black bullet hole, bore the scarlet imprint of—a Spider!

Slowly Wentworth walked from the room. At the door he said wearily: "I think this will be the end of the Keystone Massa-cres. I'll leave it to you, Charley, to tell Susan about—her father."

And while the two men watched in silence, the Spider stepped out of the room.